REHANA, ZUBAIDHA AND OTHER POOR SOULS...

(a collection of short stories)

By

BALAJI RAMAKRISHNAN

Rehana, Zubaidha and other poor souls...

Rehana, Zubaidha and other poor souls...

DEDICATED

TO

MY DEAR PARENTS

First Edition
2025
Chennai, India

Copyright © Balaji Ramakrishnan 2025

3

Rehana, Zubaidha and other poor souls...

Publisher Details

Notion Press India office is at No. 7, Red Cross Road, Egmore, Chennai, Tamil Nadu 600008

Notion press Delhi office at 3rd Floor, 6768, Chandra Bhavan, New, Nehru Place, Delhi - 110019.

Overseas

Notion Press USA office at 800 West El Camino Real #180, California USA 94040

(also available on Flipkart and Amazon)

TABLE OF CONTENTS

1. THE REVENGE GONE WRONG
2. THE HITTITE'S COUNT
3. THE BELL AND THE TIDE
4. REHANA- LONGING TO BE LOVED
5. THE UNPROMISED LOVE
6. PUPPY LOVE – THE BEGINNING
7. PUPPY LOVE – THE END
8. THE NEEM'S SONG
9. THE UNSPOKEN LOVE OF KARUPAIYYAH
10. THE BOY UNDER THE WHISPERING WILLOW
11. A WALK IN THE COLD HILLS
12. THE LANTERN OF LOST LOVE
13. PANCHAKALYANI'S LAMENT
14. THE KEEPER'S SON
15. THE REAL HEAVEN
16. FORGIVENESS
17. THE WHISPERS OF AVADI
18. THE LUNAR WHISPER – PART ONE
19. THE LUNAR WHISPER – PART TWO
20. JP SIR – RISE AND FALL
21. ZUBAIDHA – AN ANDAMAN ELEGY
22. THASOS – BLOOD AND STONE
23. LIFE – A GIFT TO BE LIVED
24. SHADOWS OF LONG ISLAND

Rehana, Zubaidha and other poor souls...

1. THE REVENGE GONE WRONG

The clock ticks loud, a hammer in my head,
Each second a reminder, of the words left unsaid.
A hollow space where love should reside,
Replaced by this anger, I can't seem to hide.

She faded young, a whisper in the breeze, And
you, Dad, were busy, with your work, if you
please. Each cough, each fever, a plea I held so
tight, While your attention was elsewhere,
bathed in office light.

Now, the years march on, a bitter, cruel parade,
And I'm left with this fury, a life, poorly made. I
see her face in the photos on the wall, A ghost of
a mother, you let her stand and fall.

So, I glare at your face, a stranger yet so known,
My heart, a cracked vessel, where love has never
grown. This anger simmers, a boiling, dark
despair, A constant reminder, that you were
never there.

The Madras High Court felt both intimately familiar and terrifyingly alien today. The polished mahogany, the hushed whispers, the weight of expectation in the air – these were the constants of my childhood, the backdrop to my father's illustrious career. Prakash Raj. The name resonated with respect, with victory. Today, that name echoed with a different kind of resonance for me – one of betrayal and neglect.

My hands, usually steady, trembled as I adjusted my advocate's gown. Fifteen years. Fifteen years since my mother, Banupriya, breathed her last. Fifteen years of a simmering anger that had finally boiled over, propelling me onto this hallowed ground, not as a proud daughter, but as an adversary.

My gaze drifted towards the defendant's bench. There he sat, my father, the formidable Justice Prakash Raj. His posture was as impeccable as ever, his silver hair neatly combed, his expression unreadable. Or was it? Did I detect a flicker of something in his eyes, a shadow of the man who once lifted me onto his shoulders and told me I was his little queen?

Beside him sat Uncle Rajender, his younger brother. His usual jovial demeanor was replaced by a grim determination. He believed in his brother, I knew. He saw the accolades, the unwavering dedication to the bench. He didn't see the gaping holes in our family history, the absence that had carved a permanent scar on my soul.

Across the aisle, my maternal grandfather, Amitabh, sat ramrod straight, his eyes boring into my father with undisguised animosity. His support had been a silent, steady current beneath the surface of my legal studies, a constant reminder of the injustice he felt my mother had suffered. His whispers during my childhood, the tales of my mother's fading health and my father's preoccupation with work, had been carefully planted seeds that had finally blossomed into this legal battle.

The courtroom doors creaked open, and Judge Radharavi entered, his presence commanding immediate silence. He was a man known for his impartiality, his keen intellect. Today, his gaze held a particular weight as it swept over the players in this tragic drama.

"Court is in session," the court officer announced.

My heart hammered against my ribs. This was it. The culmination of years of planning, of meticulously gathering evidence, of steeling myself for this confrontation.

My opening statement was delivered with a voice that surprised even myself – clear, strong, and unwavering. I painted a picture of my mother's slow decline, the early signs dismissed, the doctor's visits postponed. I spoke of the gap between the initial complaints and the eventual diagnosis, the crucial time lost while my father was engrossed in complex cases in Delhi, Kolkata, Chennai.

I presented the medical reports, stark black and white documents that chronicled the timeline of my mother's illness. The dates of tests, the dates of consultations, the glaring void between them – these were the irrefutable proof of my father's neglect. Each date I read aloud felt like a blow against the carefully constructed image of the perfect judge.

Uncle Rajender, in his defense, argued that my father was a man of his time, a man burdened by the responsibility of providing for his family. "In India," he declared, his voice resonating through the silent courtroom, "the weight of the family rests on the man's shoulders. He works tirelessly to feed his loved ones, and sometimes, in that relentless pursuit, other needs get unintentionally overlooked."

His words hung in the air, a justification for a societal norm that had cost me my mother. A wave of anger washed over me. Unintentional? Overlooked? My mother's life was not something to be casually overlooked.

Then came the moment I had been both dreading and anticipating. I presented the evidence of my childhood injury, a minor fall that had resulted in a week-long hospital stay. My voice trembled slightly as I described my father's constant presence by my bedside, his worried face, his unwavering attention.

"For seven days," I stated, my gaze fixed on my father, "my father, the esteemed

Justice Prakash Raj, remained by my side, neglecting his crucial cases, his demanding schedule. He held my hand, he told me stories, he made sure I had everything I needed. He told me, Your Honour, that I was the most precious thing in his world."

A pin could have dropped in the silence that followed. I saw a flicker of pain in my father's eyes, a ghost of the love I once knew.

"And yet," I continued, my voice gaining strength, "when his wife, his life partner, the mother of his child, lay sick, those same urgent cases, that same demanding schedule, took precedence. My grandfather, Your Honour," I turned towards Amitabh, "loved his daughter with the same intensity, the same unwavering devotion that my father showed me during my trivial illness. But that love, that care, was not reciprocated by the man who had pledged to cherish her."

My father's defense was subdued. He spoke of the pressures of his profession, the demands on his time, the belief that my mother was receiving the best possible care.

But his words lacked conviction, overshadowed by the stark contrast of his actions during my childhood illness.

Then came the memory of the conversation I had overheard, a conversation that had solidified my resolve. It was between my parents, a few months before my mother's passing. Her voice, weak but firm, had reached my ears through the slightly ajar door.

"There is a woman behind every man's victory, Prakash," she had said, her voice raspy. "And I will be behind yours, even… even when I'm not physically here. Be the best judge in this country, my love. Don't let anything hold you back. I'll be alright. I'll never be a hurdle in your path to victory."

Her words, meant to be an act of selfless love, now echoed in the courtroom as a stark indictment of his priorities. Her desire for his success had inadvertently become a shield against her own needs.

Uncle Rajender, in his closing arguments, reiterated the societal pressures, the unintentional nature of the neglect. He emphasized my father's dedication as a judge, his contribution to the legal system. He painted him as a victim of circumstances, a man trapped by the demands of his profession.

But I had planted the seeds of doubt, the undeniable comparison of his actions. The love he had so readily shown his daughter, the care he had so diligently provided during a minor ailment, stood in stark contrast to the absence during his wife's more serious illness.

Judge Radharavi listened intently, his expression impassive. The weight of his decision hung heavy in the air. The courtroom was still, every breath held captive.

Finally, after what felt like an eternity, he began to speak. He acknowledged the arguments from both sides, the complexities of the situation, the societal norms that often placed the burden of breadwinning over other responsibilities.

My heart pounded in my chest. I braced myself for the inevitable, for the justification of a system that often overlooked the needs of women in the face of male ambitions.

But then, he said, "While the court acknowledges the societal pressures and the demands of the legal profession, the evidence presented highlights a stark disparity in the attention and care provided in two similar, yet vastly different, circumstances."

My breath caught in my throat. Hope, a fragile butterfly, fluttered in my chest.

"The court finds that while no malicious intent is evident, a demonstrable lack of timely medical attention contributed to the unfortunate outcome in the case of the deceased, Banupriya. However, the legal framework does not provide for the specific redress sought by the petitioner in this instance."

A wave of disappointment washed over me. Not guilty? But he had just acknowledged the neglect.

Judge Radharavi continued, his voice somber, "Therefore, while the court finds merit in the petitioner's claims regarding the disparity in care, it is constrained by the existing legal framework. The verdict is in favor of the defendant, Justice Prakash Raj."

A collective sigh swept through the courtroom. Uncle Rajender placed a hand on my father's shoulder, relief evident on his face. My grandfather's face was a mask of fury. My own emotions were a tangled mess of disappointment, a strange sense of vindication mixed with defeat.

The judge adjourned the court. People began to stir, the hushed whispers resuming, the tension slowly dissipating. But there was no movement from my father. He sat still, his gaze fixed on some unseen point in the distance.

Uncle Rajender gently shook his shoulder. "Anna? It's over. We won."

My father remained unresponsive. Uncle Rajender shook him again, a little harder this time. And then, with a slow, almost elegant slump, Justice Prakash Raj fell sideways, his head resting against the polished wood of the defendant's bench.

A collective gasp filled the courtroom. Chaos erupted. Someone shouted for a doctor. But I knew, with a chilling certainty, that it was too late.

As the paramedics rushed forward, their movements frantic, my gaze remained fixed on my father's still form. The victory he had sought, the career he had prioritized, had come at a cost far greater than he had ever imagined. And in the end, my mother, in her silent absence, had won after all. Her last words, her unwavering support, had unknowingly woven a web of guilt that had finally claimed its due. The weight of his victory, the undeniable truth of his neglect, had finally broken him.

2. THE HITTITE'S COUNT

The Hittite rides, a bronze god in the sun's harsh glare, Across the plains to Rabbah, a messenger of war. His chariot's rumble, a heartbeat in the dust, Armor gleaming, a promise of righteous, fierce disgust.

He carries not a banner, but a sealed decree, His king's own hand, a whispered irony. Uriah, warrior strong, with loyalty ablaze, Rushes headlong toward a carefully plotted maze.

His heart, a shattered vessel, though his face shows no despair, For the king's own treachery, a secret he must bear. He rides with fury, a whirlwind in his stride, To conquer that which David has already implied.

He seeks no glory, but a swift, honorable end, In Rabbah's dust, his duty he must send. He rides to meet his foe, in a dance of steel and death, Unknowing that his own end is the king's cold, cruel breath.

My sun, a brassy shield above, beat down on
Rabbah's wall,
Each stone a silent, sweating mouth,
awaiting its downfall.

The dust, a serpent in the wind, it choked
and stung and bit,
But we, the hounds of David's war, held fast,
where we were writ.

Uriah, they called me then, from Heth's far-
reaching land,
A warrior with calloused hands and loyalty
at command.

Among the thirty chieftains bold, my axe
had sung its song,
And Joab, David's kin, our lead, where
fierce the fight and long.

He, Joab, with his grizzled beard and eyes
that missed no sign,
His uncle's shadow on the field, strategy his
design.
And David, in Jerusalem, upon his palace
height, Awaited news, the ebb and flow, of
darkness and of light.

We bled beneath those burning skies, while
he in cool repose,
Received the tidings carried swift, of victory
or woes.

A king's life, held apart from grime, from
sweat and anguished cry,
While we, his instruments of might, beneath
a ruthless sky,

Prepared to breach those stubborn walls, to
paint the sands with red,
For kingdom's sake, for David's name, the
living and the dead.

Then came the summons, strange and swift,
a rider through the night,
"Uriah, son of Heth, the King desires your
very sight."

My brow furrowed, confusion's cloud, a
whisper in the air,
What need had David now of me, while
battle raged out there?

I sought out Joab, told the news, his gaze
grew sharp and keen,
A fleeting shadow crossed his face, had he
some inkling seen?

"Go then, Uriah," was his word, his voice a
grumbled sound,
"Attend the king, and swiftly back, where
duty can be found."

Jerusalem, a polished gem, that shimmered
in the haze,
A world removed from splintered shields
and battle's fiery blaze.

The palace gleamed, a marble dream, where
fountains sang their tune,
And David walked upon his roof, beneath
the silent moon.

It was from there, they later said, his gaze
had chanced to fall,
Upon a sight, forbidden fruit, that brought
about my fall.

Bathsheba, wife, devoted claimed, of this
my weary soul,
Bathed in the courtyard's private depths,
beyond her own control,

Had caught the eye of slumbering lust, in
David's aging breast,

A king's desire, a fatal fire, that put my faith
to test.

He sent, they say, a silent hand, to bring her
to his side,
And in that gilded cage of sin, her honor cast
aside.

My Bathsheba, the promised dove, the
solace of my heart,
Had yielded to the royal whim, and played a
traitor's part.

Weeks passed, perhaps, the siege held on,
my thoughts with her remained,
A warrior's longing, deep and true, for
comforts to be gained.

Then came a second urgent call, through
Joab, stern and brief,
"The King requires your presence now," it
brought a strange relief.

To leave the fray, to see her face, to chase
away the fear,
That lingered with each whispered tale, that
pierced my soldier's ear.

I stood before the King, his eyes, though
aged, still held command,
He spoke of Rabbah, of the fight, the
progress in the land.

I answered true, recounted all, the losses and
the gains,
The weary men, the crumbling walls, the
blood upon the plains.

He feigned concern, inquired with care, of
burdens I might bear,
Then, with a smile too bright, too false, he
offered this to share:

"Go to your house, Uriah, rest, embrace
your loving wife,
The stress of war can dim the soul, rekindle
now your life."

My heart leaped up, a joyful bird, then
faltered in its flight,
A soldier's code, a whispered voice,
declared it was not right.

"The Ark of God, my lord, resides within a
canvas fold,
My comrades sleep beneath the stars, their
stories yet untold.

Shall I, then, feast on silken sheets, and seek
a woman's grace,
While brothers fight and brave men fall, in
this forsaken place?

As surely as your spirit lives, I cannot grant
such plea,
To rest in comfort, while they strive, is not
the man in me."

A flicker crossed his royal gaze, a shadow,
quickly gone,
He praised my loyalty, my zeal, until the
early dawn.

Then pressed me once again to go, to seek
my wife's embrace,
And when I stood my ground once more, a
new plan took its place.

"Tomorrow then," the king declared, a
sealed scroll in his hand,
"You shall return to Joab's camp, according
to my command.

Take him this message, bear it swift," his
eyes avoided mine,

And I, a fool for king and crown, obeyed his
dark design.

The scroll felt heavy in my hand, a mission
to fulfill,
Unknowing that within its folds, my destiny
lay still.

Back to the lines, the smoky air, the
comrades grimy-faced,
I sought out Joab, gave the scroll, no hint of
fear embraced.

He broke the seal, his weathered face, grew
pale beneath the sun,
His lips moved silently, his breath, caught
short, the damage done.

He looked at me, a pitying gaze, a sorrow in
his stare,
And in that moment, something cold, began
to bloom in there,

Within my heart, a chilling doubt, a whisper
of deceit,
But loyalty, a binding chain, would not
allow retreat.

The next day's dawn, a crimson stain, upon
the eastern sky,
The final push, the walls to breach, where
many men would die.

Joab addressed the troops, his voice, a
gravelly command,
"Uriah, with your bravest men, shall lead
this valiant band!"

A thrill shot through me, warrior's pride, to
stand within the fore,
To strike the blow that ends the siege, and
spill the enemy's gore.

I mounted up, my warhorse strong, his
muscles tight and lean,
My axe gleamed bright, a hungry mouth, for
vengeance yet unseen.

We charged the breach, a roaring wave,
against the stubborn stone,
The clash of steel, the dying screams, a
symphony of groan.

I fought like ten, a whirlwind's wrath, my
fury knew no bounds,
Cleaving through ranks, a crimson path,
across the ravaged grounds.

Then, in the thickest of the fight, I saw the
shifting line,
My flanking troops, pulled back, away, no
plan of theirs or mine.

An open path, a deadly trap, was laid before
my eyes,
And in that flash of brutal truth, the king's
treachery did rise.

The sealed scroll, Joab's stricken face,
the king's insistent plea, The puzzle pieces
clicked in place,

my certain destiny. A bitter smile touched
my lips, no anger, just regret,
 For misplaced trust, for broken oaths, a life
that was not yet,

Complete, with children at my knee, and
Bathsheba's warm hand,
Instead, a king's vile selfish need, defiling
all the land.

I saw Joab watching, his anguish etched
upon his brow,
He knew, he understood it all, the reason for
it now.

I spurred my steed, a final surge, toward the
waiting foe,
A hundred blades, a shower of spears, where
I was meant to go.

No fear I felt, just noble rage, against the
tyrant's whim,
To meet my end with warrior's grace, upon
this bloody brim.

I cut them down, left and right, a dance of
death and might,
Their numbers vast, but courage strong,
burned in my fading light.

The walls of Rabbah crumbled then, the
victory was won,
But for Uriah, son of Heth, his earthly race
was run.

Badly wounded, I tumbled down, near
Joab's muddy feet,
My breath came hard, my vision blurred, the
taste of iron sweet.

He knelt beside me, grief-filled eyes, his
voice a whispered plea, "Forgive me, friend,
I could not stop, this cruel atrocity.

"I shook my head, no blame I held, for him,
the loyal soul,
"Tell David this," I gasped for air, "I fought
to reach the goal.

Tell him Uriah died a man, a warrior, brave
and true,"
My hand went limp, my spirit fled, beneath
the fading blue.

Joab remained, his head bowed low, above
the Hittite's form,
A great man lost, a king's dark stain, upon
the battle's storm.

The price of lust, the cost of pride, a
kingdom built on lies,
And Uriah, in silent death, judged them with
sightless eyes.

Rabbah was taken, as foretold, the victory
was claimed,
But in the heart of Joab's grief, a different
war was framed.

The memory of Uriah's smile, that final,
knowing glance,
A sacrifice to royal sin, a warrior's last,
brave dance.

3. THE BELL AND THE TIDE

The salt spray kissed my face, a welcome change
From soapy floors and hymns that felt so
strange. No more the church, its shadowed,
judging eye, No more the whispers as the days
went by. Philomena, they called me, orphan girl
and meek, But now I stand, a future I can speak.

My heart, a battlefield where love had bled, Now
mends beneath a roof where dreams are bred.
My warrior found me, broken, lost and torn,
And vowed to build a haven, a new morn. He,
strong and gentle, like the oak tree tall, Will
stand beside me, through rise and fall.

And soon, a babe will grace our humble door,
Beside the harbor's edge, where seagulls soar. A
little hut, the lighthouse in its gaze, We'll build a
life of love, in peaceful ways. No bishops, priests,
or nuns will have their say, We'll be our own
family, come what may.

The salt-laced wind whipped
Philomena's dark hair across her face as she
stood by the window. Below, the churning

turquoise of the sea met the jagged black rocks that ringed St. Philomena's Island. For twenty-two years, this view had been the frame around her world. The ancient stone walls of the orphanage, built centuries ago by some forgotten order, felt both like a sanctuary and a cage.

Inside, the familiar rhythm of the orphanage day unfolded. The clatter of breakfast dishes, the murmur of prayers, the distant chanting from the old stone church. Philomena could hear Mother Superior Angelina's firm, measured footsteps on the creaking floorboards. The woman was a force, her presence radiating an unwavering piety that had shaped Philomena's entire existence. A piety, Philomena increasingly feared, planned to swallow her whole.

Angelina envisioned Philomena in a habit, another black-clad figure gliding through the hallowed halls, her life dedicated to God. "You have a calling, child," she'd say, her voice a low, resonant hum. "You were brought here, a gift to St. Philomena. This is your destiny."

But Philomena's destiny felt different. It smelled not of incense and old stone, but of woodsmoke and freshly turned earth. She dreamed of a small house with sunlight streaming through the windows, of laughter echoing in the rooms, of a hand held tightly in hers. She yearned for the common life, the joy and sorrow of the everyday world that existed just beyond the island's shores.

Her sisters in the orphanage, the girls she'd grown up with, understood. Nuns like Sister Agnes, with her kind eyes and gentle smile, would often pat her hand and say, "Don't you worry, child. The Lord works in mysterious ways. Maybe your path leads you beyond these walls." They saw the vibrant spirit in Philomena, the yearning for connection that wouldn't be quenched by a life of solemn vows.

Philomena knew her story. Mother Superior had never kept it a secret. Foundling. Abandoned. Placed as an infant on the cold earth of the graveyard, next to the ancient church, twenty-two years ago. Mother Superior herself had discovered her, a tiny bundle wrapped in rags, miraculously alive. St. Philomena's, she believed, had received her namesake in the most literal way.

Sundays were both a comfort and a torment. The high, vaulted ceilings of the church echoed with the hymns, the stained glass casting kaleidoscopic patterns on the worn stone floor. And there, usually in the third pew from the front, was Antony.

He was a year or two older than her, a young man with kind eyes and a hesitant smile. The only son of the wealthy Gonzales family, who owned the largest fishing fleet on the neighboring island. Philomena had never spoken a word to him, just watched him, a silent observer of his quiet devotion. His presence sparked a warmth in her chest, a feeling she couldn't name but desperately craved.

She knew, from the shy glances he occasionally directed her way, that Antony noticed her too. But the chasm between them felt vast. She, an orphan of the church, and he, the scion of a prominent family.

One Tuesday afternoon, Philomena was on her knees, polishing the smooth, cool stones of the church floor. The scent of beeswax filled the air. The heavy oak doors creaked open, and Antony stepped inside. Father Benjamin, the aging priest, greeted him warmly. "Antony, my son! A blessed birthday to you." They spoke for a few minutes, Father Benjamin offering his blessings, before the priest shuffled off towards the vestry.

Antony stood for a moment, seemingly hesitant, then turned his gaze towards Philomena. Her heart hammered against her ribs. He was closer than she'd ever been.

He cleared his throat. "Philomena, isn't it?" His voice was deeper than she imagined.

She could only nod, her hands stilling on the polishing cloth.

"I… I saw you here," he continued, his cheeks flushing slightly. "Every Sunday."

A shy smile touched her lips. "And I you." The words were barely a whisper.

That brief encounter was the spark. Their meetings began furtively, under the watchful gaze of the ancient tombstones in the graveyard. They'd talk in hushed tones, the sea whispering its secrets to the shore. Antony spoke of his dreams of modernizing his father's fleet, of his love for the sea. Philomena spoke of her yearning for a life beyond the orphanage walls, her dreams of a family. They discovered a shared love for the island, for the wild beauty of the coastline, for the stories whispered by the wind.

Their connection deepened with each stolen moment. Antony's touch, when their hands brushed, sent shivers down her spine. He was everything she'd ever dreamed of – kind, gentle, his eyes filled with a warmth that mirrored her own longing.

But their secret couldn't stay hidden forever. Mother Superior's gaze, always sharp, grew colder. Whispers reached her ears. One evening, as Philomena was returning from a late errand, Angelina intercepted her in the dimly lit corridor.

"Philomena," her voice was low and stern. "I hear you've been keeping company."
Philomena's heart sank. She could only nod, shame washing over her.

"With Antony Gonzales," Mother Superior stated, her voice devoid of warmth. "This must stop, child. It is not fitting. Your path lies here, within these walls."

Philomena pleaded, her voice trembling. "But Mother Superior, I love him. And he loves me."

"Love is a fleeting sentiment, child. Devotion to God is eternal." Angelina's words were like stones. "He is of the world, and you... you belong here. Consider this a warning."

But warnings couldn't extinguish the fire that burned between them. They continued to meet, their moments together tinged with fear and a desperate desire to cling to their fragile happiness.

The inevitable explosion came on a Sunday, during mass. As the congregation knelt for communion, Antony's father, a stern-faced man with a powerful presence, strode purposefully towards the altar. He stopped before Antony, his voice booming through the hushed church.

"Antony! Is this true? Are you… are you courting this… this orphan girl?"

The air crackled with tension. Every eye in the church turned towards the drama unfolding. Antony stood, his face pale but resolute. He looked at Philomena, his gaze filled with love and determination.

"Yes, Father. I love Philomena."

His father's face contorted in fury. "You will not disgrace this family! She is nothing but a pauper, raised by charity! If you persist in this folly, you are no son of mine. You will be disinherited, stripped of your name, your inheritance – everything!"

The words hung in the air, heavy and suffocating. Philomena felt a wave of shame and despair wash over her.

The next morning, the bells of St. Philomena's didn't toll for a wedding. Instead, Philomena, dressed in a simple cotton dress, met Antony at the registration office on the mainland. Their vows were whispered, their signatures shaky. They were married, with nothing but their love and the clothes on their backs.

Their happiness, though intense, was fragile. Antony found work at the nearby shipyard, the labor grueling, the pay meager. They rented a small room above a noisy tavern, the sounds of drunken revelry often seeping through the thin walls. Philomena, now carrying their child, worked odd jobs, mending nets and cleaning houses.

Yet, amidst the hardship, their love remained a constant beacon. Every evening, they would walk hand-in-hand to the old lighthouse tower that stood sentinel on the cliff overlooking the sea. They'd lean against the cool stone, watching the waves crash against the rocks, the salt spray on their faces. Those moments, bathed in the golden light of the setting sun, were their sanctuary, a reminder of the love that had defied convention and consequence.

One evening, Philomena was alone in their tiny room, mending a tear in Antony's work shirt. A disheveled man, his clothes stained with grime and oil, burst through the door, his eyes wide with panic.

"Are you Philomena? Antony's wife?" he gasped. "There's been an accident at the shipyard. He's badly hurt."

Fear gripped Philomena's heart like a vise. She followed the man, her breath catching in her throat, to the small St. Philomena's hospital on the mainland. But as they reached the entrance, a stern-faced nurse blocked their way.

"We have instructions," she said, her voice cold. "Mr. Gonzales is not to be admitted."
Philomena's blood ran cold. She understood. Antony's father.

They tried other hospitals, but the word had spread. Doors were slammed in their faces. Finally, they carried Antony back to their small room, his breathing shallow, his face ashen. Philomena cradled him in her arms, her tears falling onto his forehead. He died before dawn, his last breath a whisper of her name.

Drenched in Antony's blood, her womb heavy with their unborn child, Philomena was consumed by a grief so profound it threatened to shatter her. She knew where Antony belonged – in the earth of St. Philomena's, the island that held their love story.

She walked through the pre-dawn darkness, Antony's lifeless form heavy in her arms, back to the island, to the familiar gates of the orphanage. She hammered on the heavy wooden doors, her voice hoarse with desperation.

"Please! He's dead! Let me bury him in the graveyard. It's all I ask."

Mother Superior appeared, her face etched with sorrow but firm. "I am sorry, child. But it cannot be. He forfeited his right to consecrated ground. And you... you chose your path."

Denied even this final solace, Philomena's despair turned to a cold, hard resolve. Dragging Antony's body, her strength fueled by a love that transcended death, she made her way to the graveyard. The pickaxe leaned against the stone wall, left by a groundskeeper. The wet earth was heavy, resistant. As she swung the pickaxe, the first sharp pangs of labor tore through her.

She didn't stop. She dug, her hands raw and bleeding, the sweat mingling with the tears streaming down her face. Finally, the hole was deep enough. With a final surge of strength, she lowered Antony into the earth.

As the first rays of dawn painted the sky, Philomena lay beside his makeshift grave, her body wracked with pain. She felt the final, agonizing push, and a small, whimpering cry pierced the stillness. A daughter. Antony's daughter.

Holding the tiny, fragile life against her chest, Philomena closed her eyes. The pain receded, replaced by a profound weariness. She saw Antony's face, his loving smile. The sound of the tide washing against the shore, the mournful tolling of the distant church bell, faded into silence. Mother and father, reunited in the embrace of St. Philomena's earth, their love story etched forever in the lonely graveyard by the sea.

4. REHANA - LONGING TO BE LOVED

The sun, a hammer, beat the soil, same as my heart. Another day, another toil, another weary start. Six mouths to feed, besides my own, Each calloused hand, a seed we've sown.

Mother's eyes, like sea-worn stone, Hold no warmth, no love I've known. Father's ghost, a whispered name, Left us with shadows, and with shame.

But then a whisper, a distant bell, A relative, a story to tell. A match, a husband, far away, A life beyond this dusty bay.

My head a-spin, my heart takes flight, Of feasts and music, pure delight! No more the sun-baked earth to till, But laughter bright, and drinks that spill.

Marriage, they say, a grand affair, With flavours new, beyond compare. A chance to leave this endless grind, A different world, a different mind. Oh, distant land, my hopeful call, Away from here, I give my all.

The rain was a constant companion in Rehana's young life. It hammered against the thatched roof of their small house in the Andaman Islands, turning the ground outside into a slick, brown morass. Eight months of the year, the downpour was relentless, a drumming rhythm that seeped into your bones. Inside, the mud floor was perpetually damp, cool and clinging to bare feet. Sometimes, in the early mornings, immense footprints would mar the soft earth outside – silent testament to the lumbering elephants that roamed the fringes of their village, gentle giants who, perhaps understanding their shared poverty, never bothered them.

Rehana was the eldest, a responsibility thrust upon her with the arrival of each new sibling. Five pairs of eyes followed her around their small plot of land, a constant reminder of the mouths she helped to feed. Their farm wasn't much – a patch carved out of the dense foliage where they coaxed meager crops from the stubbornly fertile soil. She worked tirelessly alongside her mother, Zubaida, her small hands hardened by the rough work.

Abdul Karim, her father, had a way with the fishing nets and a smile that could momentarily chase away the grey skies. He loved Rehana, that much was clear, his calloused hand gently ruffling her hair, a softness absent in his dealings with her mother. But that smile, like the brief spells of sunshine, was fleeting. He'd found that sunshine elsewhere, another woman in a neighboring village, leaving Zubaida with six children and a heart turned to stone.

Zubaida's anger was a silent, simmering thing, directed less at the absent Abdul and more at the tangible presence of his eldest daughter. Rehana became the receptacle for all the bitterness and resentment, each task assigned with a curt word, each mistake met with a sharp reprimand. There were no smiles in their house, not anymore. Zubaida's face was a mask of grim determination, etched with the lines of hardship and betrayal.

Rehana found solace in the routine, the predictable cycle of planting, weeding, harvesting. It was hard work, back-breaking at times, but it was a tangible effort with a tangible result. The animals too, were a constant presence. Buffaloes lowed in the makeshift shed, goats bleated incessantly, and the frantic squawking of hens and ducks filled the air. In the wet season, when the low-lying land flooded, the animals were sometimes herded inside their already cramped home, adding another layer of chaos and a distinct barnyard aroma.

School had been her only escape, a small building with a leaky roof where she'd learned to read and write. She'd even made it to class ten, a significant achievement in their village. But the final exams had been her undoing. The 'Fail' stamped on her certificate felt like another weight added to her already burdened shoulders.

Her dreams were simple, born out of the drudgery of her daily life. She longed for a loving hand, a gentle voice, someone to take her away from the endless toil, away from the smell of animal dung and damp earth. She dreamt of dry floors and quiet nights, a life where her worth wasn't measured in the number of weeds she pulled.

Then, news arrived. A proposal. From Rangat, a coastal town a hundred miles away, a place that sounded impossibly grand.

The alliance was brought by a distant relative, whispers of a decent young man, a driver. Rehana's heart, buried under layers of exhaustion and resignation, fluttered with a fragile hope. She accepted immediately, the prospect of escape outweighing the fear of the unknown.

The Nikah was a rushed affair, dictated by the tides and the available boats. Within days, Rehana found herself on a small, overcrowded ferry, the familiar shores of her island receding in the distance. The 'baraat', a small group of relatives, accompanied her, their faces a mixture of anticipation and concern. Rangat was indeed bigger, bustling with a chaotic energy that was both intimidating and exhilarating.

But her dreams, so carefully nurtured, began to fray at the edges almost immediately. Asraf, her husband, was a thin, nervous man with perpetually stained teeth from chewing paan. His eyes held a shifty quality, and the warmth she'd hoped for was conspicuously absent. The nights were painful, not just physically, but emotionally. His touch felt perfunctory, devoid of affection.

He was, as the whispers in the household suggested, a puppet. His parents, having embraced the modern trend of remarriage, had left him in the care of his paternal grandmother, a formidable woman with a sharp tongue and even sharper eyes. Asraf worked as a jeep driver, his income supplemented by the cheap liquor he often indulged in. The smell of alcohol and betel nut became another unwelcome constant in Rehana's life.

Her days in Rangat mirrored her life back home, just within different walls. The grandmother, a stern matriarch, woke her before dawn, the sky still a deep indigo. Chores awaited – preparing meals for Asraf's 'fufu' (father's sister), 'fufa' (father's sister's husband), and their noisy brood of children. Rehana toiled from morning till night, the damp earth replaced by the rough stone of the courtyard, the animal smells replaced by the pungent odor of spices and frying oil.

Then came the news of her pregnancy, a flicker of hope in the oppressive routine. The grandmother, surprisingly, softened slightly. Perhaps a grandchild would solidify Asraf's place in the family, keep him from drifting further. But Asraf remained distant, his visits to the local liquor shop more frequent than his conversations with Rehana.

When the time came, she returned to her mother's house, the familiar rain-soaked landscape a strange comfort. She delivered a girl, Resham, a tiny bundle of hope amidst the persistent dampness. Asraf visited a few times, his eyes vacant, his interest clearly waning. Then, he simply stopped coming. The whispers carried on the village wind confirmed her fears – he'd run off with another woman, a widow from a nearby settlement.

Rehana was back where she started, her dreams reduced to ashes. Zubaida's words were as cold as the Andaman winter winds, a constant refrain of "I told you so" unspoken but palpable in her every glance. Tears were a luxury Rehana couldn't afford. She had Resham to feed, another mouth in a house already struggling. The familiar rhythm of farm work enveloped her again, her back aching, her hands raw. She held onto Resham, her small daughter a fragile anchor in the storm of her life, silently praying for another escape route.

Ten years passed. Resham grew, a bright spark in their otherwise bleak existence. At a cousin's wedding, a rare occasion for celebration, Rehana saw him. Bala. He was a Hindu, a fact that raised eyebrows in their predominantly Muslim community. He wasn't handsome in the conventional sense, but his eyes held a kind warmth she hadn't seen in a long time. He was an Engineer, his skin dark and weathered, his hands strong.

He was divorced, a story he shared without shame. Rehana, emboldened by a desperate need for connection, told him her own story, the failures and the heartaches laid bare under the tropical sun. They went fishing in the backwaters, the quiet lapping of water against their small boat a peaceful counterpoint to the usual noise of her life. Her siblings tagged along, their laughter echoing across the still water. For the first time in years, Rehana felt a lightness in her chest.

They decided to marry, a quiet ceremony witnessed by close family. They moved to Wellington, a town in Tamil Nadu, a world away from the familiar shores of the Andamans. Life was simple, but filled with a quiet joy. Then, the news came – Rehana was diabetic. She'd known it for a while, a nagging thirst and frequent urination, but she'd ignored it, too preoccupied with survival to consider the long-term consequences.

Her mother, the stoic Zubaida, surprised her. The distance seemed to melt away the years of bitterness. Daily phone calls bridged the thousand miles, Zubaida's voice, once sharp and critical, now soft with concern. But the newfound connection was tragically short-lived. Zubaida passed away suddenly, a heart attack, leaving Rehana with a grief so profound it felt like a physical blow. She couldn't go back for the funeral, the distance and the expense insurmountable. The guilt gnawed at her, a constant ache alongside her grief.

Bala yearned for a child. They decided to try artificial reproductive techniques. They were warned about the risks, about how the hormone injections could exacerbate Rehana's diabetes, but their desire for a child outweighed their fears. The treatment took a toll. Rehana's kidneys began to struggle. During the delivery, the glucose fluids administered worsened her diabetes drastically. Her vision blurred, her left eye slowly succumbing to the damage. But then, Roza arrived, another daughter, a tiny miracle.

A promotion for Bala brought them to Mumbai. The city was a cacophony of sounds and lights, a stark contrast to the quiet life they'd built. Rehana was happy, or at least, she pretended to be. She hid her discomfort, the increasing blurriness in her remaining eye, the constant fatigue. Her diabetes was wreaking havoc. Her vision was fading fast, distances blurring into indistinct shapes. Her kidneys were failing. Roza, barely three, was too young to understand her mother's illness.

Bala, watching his wife slowly slip away, desperately sought a transfer back to the Andaman Islands. He wanted her to be surrounded by her siblings, for Resham to be with her mother in her final days. The transfer came through. The day they were supposed to leave arrived, heavy with a bittersweet anticipation.

That night, Rehana struggled to breathe. Panic filled the small apartment. Bala, his face etched with fear, carried her to the waiting vehicle. On the way to the hospital, Rehana's breath came in ragged gasps. She reached for Bala's hand, her grip weak. "Take care of Resham too," she whispered her voice barely audible, "Love her like your own." Then, with a final sigh, her toils were over. The rain, though miles away, felt like a familiar dirge. Bala was left alone, again, the love of his life extinguished like a fragile flame.

5. THE UNPROMISED LOVE

A scrap of fur, a wisp of fear, That's all I was, just yesterday, it's clear. A lonely pup, with paws so small, Lost in the world, I'd seen it all. My mother's warmth, a fading dream, Life was a howl, a silent scream.

Then came a hand, a gentle touch, A kind embrace, I loved it much. A family vast, a boisterous crowd, Twenty children, laughing loud. They call me Appu, a name so new, And in their eyes, a future grew.

This grand old house, my brand new start, A place for me, a loving heart. I'll chase the ball, and leap and bound, With joyful barks, echoing 'round. Though lost my past, I'll look ahead, This family's love, my heart has fed.

My loyalty now, I pledge with pride, I'll guard this place, where I reside. A stray no more, a happy soul, In this great family, I've found my whole. For Appu now, the journey's bright, Filled with love, and pure delight.

My life began in the dust and shadows, a fleeting existence between the scuttling paws of other strays. Then, the scent of something warm and inviting drew me closer – a cluster of small houses huddled together, a chaotic symphony of human voices always spilling out. This was the domain of a sprawling family, twenty souls crammed into four small dwellings, bordered by the fragrant chaos of guava, mango, and the sharp prickle of bougainvillea.

I was just a scrap of fur and bones then, a pup of a nameless mother who had wandered off and never returned. Hunger was a constant companion, gnawing at my belly. My earliest memories are of furtive glances towards those houses, of the tantalizing aroma of cooked food drifting on the breeze. It was the children who first noticed me, their bright eyes following my hesitant movements.

Chitra was different. Even amongst the noisy throng of cousins and siblings, her kindness radiated like the afternoon sun. She was one of three siblings who showed me the most affection – Chitra, Balaji, and Priya.

She called me Appu with love. While the others, spurred on by the stern pronouncements of the grandfather, would shoo me away with shouts and the occasional thrown pebble, Chitra offered scraps. Not the discarded bones and gristle of the others, but morsels of rice still warm, pieces of roti torn into manageable bits, sometimes even a sliver of fish. She loved me more, I knew it in the gentle way she spoke to me, the soft scratch behind my ears that sent shivers of contentment down my spine.

Their games became a part of my young life. Balaji and Priya, full of boundless energy, would chase each other around the houses, their laughter echoing in the enclosed space. I would try to join in, my clumsy puppy paws tripping over roots and stones, my tail wagging furiously. I remember one such game vividly. Balaji, in his haste, tumbled right onto me. A sharp, searing pain shot through my small body, and I yelped, a warm dampness spreading beneath me. After that, I learned to keep a safer distance during their boisterous play, watching from the shade of a frangipani tree, a wary observer.

With regular meals, though always outside the threshold, I started to fill out, my ribs no longer so prominent. The hesitant pup transformed into a young bitch, drawing the attention of the other street dogs, their scent a mixture of bravado and desperation. The grandfather, a man with a booming voice and a perpetually furrowed brow, would erupt in anger at the sight of my suitors. "These children!" he'd bellow, his gaze sweeping over Balaji, Priya, and the other youngsters. "Feeding this creature, bringing all the riffraff to our doorstep!"

Inevitably, the change came. A heaviness settled in my belly, a quiet stirring of life within. I found myself seeking out secluded spots, digging shallow nests in the earth. I gave birth to a pup as black as the night sky, a tiny creature that whimpered and nuzzled blindly. But its life was short, a fragile flame extinguished too soon.
The next time, there was only one. A soft, brown bundle of fur, she was different from her dark sibling. Fluffy and energetic, she was a whirlwind of puppy antics, her playful nips and clumsy tumbles eliciting coos of delight from the family. Even the usually

gruff grandfather's lips would twitch into a faint smile when she tottered near. My pup, unlike me, was sometimes allowed fleeting moments inside their homes, quickly ushered out by an exasperated aunt or uncle. She would learn, as I had, the invisible boundary, the unspoken rule that dictated our place was outside.

My sanctuary became the cement park bench in front of Chitra's house. It was a solid, cool presence, a relic from their past, brought from their old home, a detail I overheard Chitra's younger uncle mention. Here, under its shade, I nursed my pups. Here, Chitra would bring my food, placing it in the dented aluminium plate that had become my own.

Beyond the cluster of houses, stretching towards the horizon, lay the abandoned paddy fields. A desolate expanse, it was a place of death and decay. Dead cows, goats – unwanted remnants of the village – were dragged there to decompose. It was a gruesome feast, but for a stray, sustenance was sustenance.

My brown daughter grew, her puppy fluff giving way to a sleek coat. She too attracted the attention of the street dogs, a constant whirlwind of chasing and snapping. The masters of the house, as I instinctively understood them to be, would chase her away with angry shouts and the swing of a broom. I began to understand that we, the stray dogs, were a source of worry, an unwanted presence. I started to ward off the other males, protecting my daughter from their advances, earning me a few moments of peace, even though it was fleeting.

Then came her turn. My daughter, too, grew heavy with life. She gave birth to a pup as black as I had been, a small, vulnerable creature that inherited the family's disdain. Three stray dogs now frequented their compound - me, my daughter, and her pup. The tolerance of the family wore thin. The little one would be kicked away from a spilled drop of milk, shooed from the shade of their verandas. But Chitra, always Chitra, would find a way. A hidden piece of bread slipped into my daughter's mouth, a gentle pat on my grandpup's head when no one else was looking.

Years blurred into a decade. Chitra blossomed into a young woman, her schoolbooks replaced by college notebooks, then by the crisp attire of someone with a job. Life continued its predictable rhythm of sun and rain, hunger and scraps.

One day, a frantic barking jolted me. It was my daughter, her cries sharp with alarm. I raced towards the sound, my heart pounding. She was at the edge of the neighbour's property, barking furiously at an open septic tank. In a flash of brown fur, she lunged, disappearing into the dark, foul-smelling water. Then, a smaller splash. My grandpup.

My barks joined my daughter's panicked cries, a desperate plea that cut through the usual household noise. The family rushed out, their faces a mixture of confusion and alarm. It was Balaji who acted first. He plunged his arm into the murky depths, his face contorted with effort. He pulled them out, one by one. My daughter, then my grandpup. Lifeless. Water streamed from their fur, the stench of the septic tank clinging to them. They were dragged to the abandoned paddy fields, their limp bodies a stark contrast to the vibrant green of the rice stalks. The emptiness they left behind was a physical ache. For days, food held no appeal, the joy of a gentle scratch gone.

It was Chitra who pulled me back from the abyss of grief. She would sit beside me on the cement bench, stroking my fur, talking to me in soft murmurs. She would coax me to eat, her gentle persistence a lifeline. Slowly, tentatively, life began to seep back into me.

Then, the harmony of the family shattered. Angry voices, hushed whispers, a palpable tension hung in the air. Chitra, my kind Chitra, had fallen in love. With someone from outside their community, a transgression in their tightly knit world. Her father's disapproval was a storm cloud over the house. Shouts echoed through the small rooms, her every move scrutinized, judged. Even Balaji, usually Chitra's ally, remained silent, his own secret love for the neighbour girl, Sharmila, a carefully guarded flame. They arranged a marriage for her, a union of their choosing. Chitra, her spirit withering, refused food, her eyes reflecting a deep, unbearable sadness. On the eve of the alliance, Balaji brought her parotta, a flatbread she loved. She didn't eat it herself, but fed it to me, piece by precious piece.

The next day, the atmosphere was suffocating. Chitra was confined to the house, her parents fearing she would elope. Despair clung to her like a shroud. Later that morning, a chilling sound cut through the quiet – a choked gasp, a thud. Near the common toilet, beneath the shade of the neem tree, lay Chitra. The acrid smell of acid hung heavy in the air. Her body convulsed, a final, desperate struggle before stillness claimed her. She was gone. My Chitra, the one who saw me, who cared, was gone. The world seemed to dim, the colours losing their vibrancy.

The family, their lives irrevocably altered, packed their belongings and left. The small houses, once filled with their cacophony, fell silent. A year passed. The seasons changed, the fruit trees blossomed and bore fruit, but the laughter was gone. I felt the slow creep of age, my steps heavier, my senses duller. One day, with a final, weary look at the empty houses, I turned and walked towards the abandoned paddy fields. The scent of decay, once repulsive, now held a strange allure. Under the vast, indifferent sky, I lay down, waiting for the end, the memories of a kind hand, a shared morsel, a silent understanding, fading with the last breaths of my life.

6. PUPPY LOVE – THE BEGINNING

In dusty lanes, where shadows played, A house stood new, a life displayed. Young Sharmi, five, with eyes so bright, Met Bala, seven, in fading light.

He, a boy of dusk, with features bold, She, a sunbeam, in stories told. From that first glance, a seed was sown, In Bala's heart, a love unknown.

A childhood crush, some might decree, A fleeting phase, for all to see. But in his mind, Sharmi took hold, A silent story, bravely told.

He watched her play, her laughter sweet, His secret kept, his heart's retreat. Through scraped knees and summer days, His love for her, in countless ways.

He never spoke, he never dared, This precious feeling, he simply shared With moonlit nights and quiet dreams, A teenage love, it always seems, A hidden treasure, safe and deep, While Sharmi, oblivious, would sleep. A boy's first love, a gentle fire, A secret flame, his heart's desire.

The camera eye settles on a landscape painted in the muted greens and browns of rural India. Paddy fields, vast and rippling, cradle a cluster of small dwellings at their edge. It is here, in this quiet corner of the world, that a story begins – a story of first love, of unspoken words, and of a heart, tender as a sapling, struggling to bloom.

Bala was seven, a boy of the earth, his skin the colour of rich soil, when Sharmi arrived. She was five, fair as a jasmine bloom, with eyes that sparkled like the monsoon rain. Her family moved into the mud-walled house next to his, its roof thatched with paddy stalks. Bala's world, a vibrant chaos of twenty family members living in four cramped dwellings within a thorny compound, suddenly found a new centre.

He watched her, a silent observer, from the moment they met. He'd smile, a shy, unconscious curve of his lips, every time their eyes met. Once, she'd tilted her head, her brow furrowed in childlike curiosity, and asked, "Why do you always smile at me, anna?" He had no answer, the words stuck in his throat, a jumble of feelings he couldn't understand, let alone articulate.

Sharmi had three older sisters, their laughter often echoing in the small compound. Bala, despite his friends calling him a recluse, would linger in the periphery, always positioning himself to catch a fleeting glimpse of her. His mother and Sharmi's mother had struck up a warm friendship and often chatted in the shaded corners of their yards. Bala, pretending to be occupied with something nearby, would always be in earshot, his eyes invariably drawn to Sharmi, her every move a source of fascination.

Summer vacations were a trial. Sharmi would disappear to her uncle's or grandparents' place for weeks, leaving a void in Bala's young world. He'd count the days, his anticipation a heavy weight in his small chest, waiting for the day her laughter would once again fill the air. He ran errands for Sharmi's family – a quick trip to the corner shop for her mother, or fetching beedis for her father. Everyone in Sharmi's family liked Bala, for his gentle nature and his ever-willing hand. They all saw him as the kind, helpful, and quiet boy next door, and not the boy who harboured a secret, burning flame.

While the other boys of the village kicked footballs or played cricket in the fields, Bala stayed close to his home, his world revolving around the confines of their compound and the sight of Sharmi's house. He had a special place, a sturdy neem tree, from where he had a clear view of her house. A silent, solitary sentinel, perched amidst the leaves, watching her life unfold.

This puppy love, innocent and pure, grew with each passing year. By the time Bala was seventeen, it had become the core of his being, a secret he carefully guarded. But there was one nagging thorn in his heart - Sharmi called him 'anna', brother. How could he ever express the love that consumed him if she saw him only as family?

Then came the day Sharmi came of age, a day marked by a tradition that sent Bala's heart soaring. The custom was that either the fiance or an uncle's son builds a special shelter, using coconut leaves, inside the house for the young girl. It was Sharmi's father, his hands resting on Bala's shoulders, who assigned him this honour. It was as if the universe had conspired to fulfill his dreams; Sharmi's father referred to him as her 'fiance'. He floated through that day, his heart in seventh heaven, a mix of joy and trepidation. Even then, Sharmi didn't stop calling him 'anna'.

The fear of rejection, a constant companion, had kept him silent for years. But the weight of his unspoken love grew too heavy to bear. One afternoon, as Sharmi was walking home from school, he followed her. His heart pounded against his ribs like a trapped bird. He stopped her, his voice barely a whisper, and poured out all that he had held back for ten long years. He spoke of his love, his unshakeable, unwavering love, and then, without waiting for her answer, he ran.

He was filled with dread, convinced that she would tell Priya, his sister, and her friend. He spent the rest of the day in anxious suspense. But as night fell, and no news reached him from Sharmi's family, he crept towards the edge of their yard, by the toilet. He found her sitting in the light of a kerosene lamp, absorbed in her studies. Summoning every ounce of courage, he asked her about the afternoon. Her reaction was not what he had anticipated. Anger flared in her eyes. She had never expected this from him, she said, her tone sharp, dismissing the love he had confessed. To her, he was and always would be, her brother.

He retreated back to his own world, his silence a stark contrast to the storm raging within. He stopped talking to Sharmi for months, burying his pain in the company of his childhood friends, Narayan, Dinesh, Ramakrishnan, and his cousin, Shankar. He found himself joining them in their usual haunts- the paddy fields, the lake, his life starting to get a jovial shade. But happiness was a distant shore, something he could see but never reach.

One day, as they sat by the lake, the friends started nudging him. Narayan, his eyes full of mischief, mentioned Sharmi's name, asking if there was something between them. Bala, unable to bear the burden any longer, spilled his heart out. He recounted his years of longing, his secret devotion, the crushing blow of her rejection. They listened, their initial surprise giving way to teasing.

The situation came to a head during the birthday celebrations of Divya, the daughter of Sharmi's elder sister, Ramya Akka. Sharmi's house was filled with the sounds of the latest film songs, adding fuel to the fire burning within Bala. His friends took full advantage of the situation, playfully mocking him about his love for Sharmi. He, in a strange way, found amusement in their teasing. He knew they were aware of what had passed between him and Sharmi that afternoon, yet he never confirmed or denied anything to them.

Sharmi, realizing that Bala had told his friends about his feelings, decided to make it clear that her feelings towards him was purely fraternal, not to him but to his friends. In front of them all, she intentionally called out, "Anna, come for the feast", twice. The word, 'anna,' was a dagger twisting in his heart, a public proclamation of the boundaries he had so desperately tried to break. Bala's face burned with shame, his carefully constructed facade crumbling around him. The world he had created for himself, the world he had hoped to share with Sharmi, lay shattered at his feet.

His long wait, his decade-long devotion, had come to an end, not with a triumphant symphony, but with this heart-wrenching, humiliating rejection. He could feel the tears welling up, a salty testament to his broken dreams. He knew that he could never face his friends again, not after this public humiliation. He knew, with a cold certainty, that he would never win Sharmi's love. The camera eye focuses on Bala's face, a picture of devastation. The image fades, leaving behind the echoes of unspoken love and the quiet heartbreak of a young boy whose world had just ended.

7. PUPPY LOVE – THE END

The chipped paint of the swing set knew their story well, Of whispered promises, a love the young could tell. Bala, sun-kissed and breathless, walked on air that day, Sharmi's "yes" a melody, chasing shadows away.

The world was muted, save the echo of her name, His teenage heart, a bonfire, fueled by love's bright flame. He saw no end to happiness, no cloud upon the blue, His Sharmi, his forever, a love both pure and new.

In a chipped tin box, his treasures lay asleep, Her broken bangles, a promise he would keep. A faded hairclip, a tiny fragile thing, Whispered tales of childhood and the joy they'd bring.

He pictured future mornings, children at their feet, Sharing stolen glances, love forever complete. He'd reached the summit, won the battle, so it seemed, Oblivious to the currents, of a life yet un-dreamed.

Bala, eighteen, his shoulders slumped, his gaze fixed on the cracked pavement as he pedals his bicycle. The sun glints off the worn frame, mirroring the dullness in his eyes. He's a ghost in his own life, a shadow flitting through the familiar streets of his small town. The vibrant colours of the houses, the boisterous chatter of children, all fade into a muted backdrop. He sees Narayan in the distance, a smirk playing on his lips, and Bala pushes harder, the chain whining in protest as he tries to outpace the memory of Sharmi's laughter, her rejection still echoing in his ears.

Three years earlier, it was different. Sharmi, fifteen, had been the sun that lit his world. Now, she was the eclipse, casting a permanent shadow over his existence. The sting of her words, the casual dismissal calling him "anna" in front of his friends, had been a brand seared onto his soul. He had retreated into himself, building walls of silence bricked with unspoken pain. College was a blur, lectures and textbooks a refuge from the turmoil within. His friends, oblivious to the quiet storm raging in his heart, saw only a quiet, hardworking student.

At home, he was the dutiful son, the loving brother to his sisters. He helped with chores, shared gentle jokes with his younger siblings. He was good, too good, almost. His sacrifices around the house were a silent testament to the love he wasn't allowed to express. His mother, bless her heart, in her daily chats with Sharmi's mother, would reveal little things—Bala's preference for certain foods, his habit of reading late into the night—not knowing that those tidbits were falling on Sharmi's ears.

Sharmi, in turn, began to notice. The bravado she had employed, the cruel indifference, began to crumble. The laughter she used to share with her friends had lost some of its joy. She couldn't quite pinpoint when it happened, but the "anna" she once flung like a taunt now felt like a lie. She saw his quiet kindness, the depth of feeling behind his averted gaze. She started watching him, waiting for him, a role reversal that was both thrilling and terrifying.

One day, the universe shifted slightly. Bala was walking with his cousin Bhuvana to the local shop. Sharmi, sitting on her porch, joined them. The whole way, there was no eye contact. Just the usual silence. A palpable tension filled the air. It was Bhuvana's chatter that cut through the awkwardness. On the return journey, Sharmi, unable to bear the silence any longer, provoked Bala. "Why don't you ever talk to me, Bala?"

He shrugged, his eyes fixed on his cracked chappals. Sharmi, emboldened by a surge of courage and a well of emotion she could no longer contain, confessed her feelings. Her words tumbled out, hesitant at first, then gaining momentum, the confession of a heart that had finally found its voice. Bala's shock was palpable. His head shot up, his eyes wide, searching hers for truth. And it was there, the love he had longed for, reflected back at him.
That day marked a new beginning. Their love was a delicate flower blooming in the dusty lanes and crowded streets. They met secretly, during street flag hoisting ceremonies, huddled together in the crowd, their hands brushing accidentally, their eyes communicating a language only they understood. Their romance was innocent, clumsy, filled with nervous giggles and stolen glances. He had tried clumsy kisses, a

shy peck on her cheek, a fumbling of lips, each moment a cherished memory. It was a love that was both intoxicating and terrifying in its fragility. They talked for hours, dreaming of their future, mapping out a life together.

They walked to their schools together, their paths diverging as they reached the school gates, and eventually, further apart when he went to college and she was in school. Their secret was well kept, whispered only to his cousins and sisters. Their world was a safe haven, a bubble of young love.
Then, the bubble burst.

Chitra, Bala's older sister, took her own life, poisoned by the despair of a love disapproved of. The acid she consumed was a corrosive force that ripped through Bala's world. His family, shattered by grief, moved away, relocating to a city twenty miles away, leaving behind the only life he had ever known. The house, the streets, the very air that held the ghosts of his memories, were all left behind.

In the three years that followed, Bala returned occasionally, his visits fuelled by the lingering ember of his love for Sharmi. He saw her, each time, a little less enthusiastic, a little more distant. But his love, like a tenacious weed, continued to grow, its roots burrowing deep into his soul. He couldn't imagine a life without her, a future devoid of her presence.

One day, he called her, his heart pounding. The voice on the other end was polite, cold, distant. "Please stop contacting me, Bala," she had said, her voice devoid of any emotion, "My marriage is fixed."

The words were like a physical blow, a punch to the gut that left him gasping for air. His world crumbled into dust. First, his sister, then his home, and now, the girl he loved, slipping away from him like sand through his fingers. He was twenty-two, barely a man, and certainly not strong enough to fight the fate that had dealt him such a crushing blow. He knew that he could not speak of this to his parents, not now, not ever.

He buried his love deep, a tombstone of silence over a burning desire. On the day of Sharmi's wedding, he couldn't sleep. The night was a long, agonizing vigil, watching the minutes tick away, each one a reminder of the life he had lost. His world, which had once been filled with colour and promise, had now been handed over to another man. It was over. His life, it seemed, was not destined to be lived, but merely endured. The young man's broken world, his love a ghost story whispered in the echoes of the past.

8. THE NEEM'S SONG

I stand, a titan, gnarled and green,
Thirty-five years, a life unseen
By eyes that knew, by hands that held,
A story whispered, a tale compelled.

I was a sapling, barely there,
Plucked from the hedge, a tender prayer.
A child's small hands, with purpose
vast, Planted me here, a future cast.

He built a kingdom, wild and free,
A miniature forest, just for me.
With grass like carpets, soft and deep,
And humble plants, their secrets to
keep.

A pond of water, still and bright,
Reflected skies, both dark and light.
Toy animals placed, a playful scene,
A woodland haven, vibrant, keen.

The others withered, vanished from
sight, But I held firm, and grew to my
height.   He climbed my limbs, a
playful sprite,   His laughter echoing,
pure and bright.

He'd swing from branches, strong and
high, A king upon his leafy sky.
With books and snacks, he'd spend the
days, Lost in stories, in sun's soft
rays.

I offered shade, a cooling grace,
A silent witness to time and space.

His adolescent heart, a burning fire,
Engraved his love, upon a branch higher,
with her name, a heart so true,
A love story whispered, of me and you.
The other trees, they matched my size,
But I, to him, held special ties.

The compound bustled, life's ebb and
flow, But all things change, as seasons
go.   One by one, the houses fell,
To dust and echo, a mournful knell.

Three vanished structures, leaving
scars, And one remains, behind rusted
bars.   The family shifted, shadows
fell,   A sister lost,
beneath my shell.

Though I could offer, just a place,
My roots, they held, in this lonely
space. He came less often, years went
by,   His tear-filled eyes, would
reach the sky.

He'd hug my trunk, with silent plea,
A past now lost, for him and me.
Then, one last visit, a farewell sigh,
He vanished then, beneath the sky.

And I remain here, strong and grand,
A lonely sentinel, in this barren land.
The heart, like bark, grows thick and
deep, As solitude, keeps secrets to
keep.

I watch the days, they come and go,
The empty road, the wind does blow.

I offered shade, to those who passed,
A silent love, that couldn't last.

The heart engraves of love and pain,
I watch the empty road in sun and rain.
I am a witness, old and true,
To life's brief moments, passing
through.

But still, a hope within me sleeps,
That one day, his return he keeps.
Perhaps he'll find, some solace here,
Beneath my branches, free from fear.

He'll see the heart, still on the limb,
And know, that I remember him.
For I am more than wood and leaf,
I am a keeper, of time and grief.

A silent home for memories kept,
A steadfast tree, where love has slept.
I stand here still, both firm and tall,
Waiting for you, that's all.

The passing seasons, a constant swirl,
Have left their mark upon this world.
But I, the Neem, will still remain,
A timeless testament to life's sweet
pain.

For even in the silence, love finds a
way, To echo softly, each and every day.
And I will whisper, in the rustling
breeze, My story of love, among the
trees.

9. THE UNSPOKEN LOVE OF KARUPAIYYAH

The sun, a brazen eye, began to gaze,
Upon the fields, in morning's hazy maze.
Karupaiyyah, a frame of skin and bone,
Sat hunched and still, upon his woven
throne. Beneath the neem, its branches
reaching high, He mourned a loss,
reflected in the sky. Kaathayi slept,
not in the straw-roofed shed, But in
the silence, where the living tread.

He'd called her name, a rough and raspy
sound, That once had drawn her, swiftly
from the ground. But silence answered,
where her footsteps fell, No clatter of
the broom, no dinner bell. The hens
remained, confined in their small space,
The goats untethered, in their wonted
place. Her coughs, the rhythmic rasp of
dying breath, Had filled the night,
presaging her death.

He knew, he knew, the fragile life was
spent, And yet, to field, his aching
steps were bent. Not heartless, no, but
fear had taken hold, To see her
lifeless, story to be told. By hurried
feet, that brought the village near,
Their murmurs of his grief, he could
not hear. He chose the fields, the
stream's soft, gentle sigh, To brush
with neem, beneath the judging sky.

The neem stick frayed, between his
weathered teeth, He saw her face, a

memory underneath. The wedding day, at
Shivan Kovil's height, A lifetime
spanned, in fading, dusty light. He'd
stood beside her, young and strong and
proud, Her vibrant smile, within a
boisterous crowd. But never words of
kindness, had he spoken To the woman
whose heart had always been unbroken.

He cursed her ways, her simple, humble
toil, Yet always found his food upon
the soil. His favorite dish, she'd
learned his taste by heart, He'd
swallowed it with silence, set apart.
No children graced their life, a barren
yield, Yet she'd remained, a rock,
within the field. A sudden sting, he
could no longer hide, Tears welled and
burned, his fierce old eyes defied.

He'd strived too well, to keep his
feelings masked, His love, a seed, that
his own hand had tasked, To lie dormant,
deep, beneath the hardened crust, Of
years of silence, and a misplaced trust.
In stoic guise, and silence's cold
embrace, He'd held her close, yet let
her fade from grace. Now gone, beyond
the reach of his embrace, He saw his
love, etched on her absent face.

He watched the sun, creep higher in the
sky, And felt a hollow ache, he
couldn't deny. The village sounds,
would soon begin to reach, And her
stillness would become a whispered
speech. He would be there, a shell of
the man he'd been, Hiding the love,

that lay unseen within. A love unspoken,
now a painful weight, Sealed by silence,
and the hand of fate.

He sat, a statue, by the paddy's edge,
The love he held, a painful, solemn
pledge. To carry it with him, through
the coming years, A symphony of silence,
laced with tears. He'd always known her,
gentle heart so pure, But words of love,
he had never spoken, of that he was
sure. And now she's gone, the chance
has slipped away, The love remains,
until his dying day. The fields lay
still, beneath the sun's harsh stare, A
testament to love, beyond compare. A
love that bloomed, in the heart of an
old man, Unspoken, yet profound, by
life's harsh plan.

The wind whispered through the trees, a
mournful sound, As Karupaiyyah's tears,
fell upon the ground. His love was
buried, as she was, deep inside, A
secret longing, he could no longer hide.
And in that moment, by the paddy's
gentle flow, He understood the depth,
of what he did not show. A love
unspoken, now a tragic tale, Of
Karupaiyyah, beneath the sun's hot veil.
He's left alone, the silence, his only
friend, And his love for Kaathayi, will
never end.

10. THE BOY UNDER THE WHISPERING WILLOW

A tiny sparrow, wings of bone, Sat perched, a boy, all on his own. Five years a whisper, life's short span, In St. Jude's cold, uncaring plan. No mother's touch, no father's hand, Just empty rooms and shifting sand.

He was a seed, left in the night, Beneath a willow's weeping light, They said, a basket, moss and hay, Abandoned child, come what may. The orphanage walls, a cage of gray, Where love had lost its hopeful sway. He yearned for warmth, a gentle gaze, A lullaby through childhood's haze. He dreamed of feasts, on laps so wide, And stories told, with love as guide. Instead, a crust, a whispered name, "A number now," erasing flame.

He'd sneak to parks, his small heart sore, And watch the happy families pour. A father's toss, a mother's kiss, A painful stab, a yearning bliss. Today he sat, by willow's grace, A tear traced down his fragile face. "Oh, God," he sighed, "I'm tired, see? Send down your angel, quick, for me. Let death's cold embrace be my release, From this hollow ache, that never cease." The wind it sighed, a mournful drone, As if the heavens heard his moan.

And there he was, beneath the wood, A figure veiled, misunderstood. No wings

of white, no harp of gold, But mortal
form, a story told. The Angel of Death,
with purpose deep, Had come to claim
what he would keep. But this young boy,
so small and frail, Had stirred a
feeling, like a gale. He saw the
anguish, raw and true, And felt a pang,
he never knew. He shed his guise, a
common man, And walked to where this
boy began.

"Hello," he said, his voice so low,
"Why all those tears, let sadness go?"
The boy looked up, his eyes so bright,
A fragile star in fading light. He told
his tale, of lonely days, Of longing
for love's gentle ways. The man he
smiled, a tender art, And offered games,
a brand new start. They played beneath
the willow shade, A friendship born, a
bond was made. The boy's small laughter,
light as air, A melody, a hopeful
prayer.

The angel watched, with troubled heart,
This innocent soul, about to depart.
His task was clear, to end the breath,
But now he fought, against cold death.
He gently led, with careful hand, To a
nearby bench, on softer stand. "The sun
feels good, let's sit here too," He
tried to change what fate had drew. But
the boy pulled back, with gentle plea,
"Please, I like it here, beneath the
tree, They say my mum, she picked this
shade, The day they left," his small
voice swayed "she left me here, when I

was born, five years ago, this very morn'."

The angel froze, his face grown pale, He knew the orchard, close as hail, Where mother lay, in silent sleep, A secret sorrow, buried deep. The wind it rose, a sudden scream, A giant branch, a deadly beam, It crashed and fell, with thunder's might, To steal the boy's light from the night. The angel surged, with strength unknown, He held the wood, above his own, His human form, it groaned and strained, As heaven's will, he now disdained.

A battle raged, in silent fight, Against the heavens, starless night. He fought with God, with all his might, To save this boy, this precious light. "He has suffered, felt no bliss, He deserves a chance, a love, a kiss!" The wind it howled, the branches cried, As angel fought with all inside. The boy, he watched, with wide-eyed fear, The struggle, growing ever near. He saw the man, his face so grim, And wondered why he fought for him. The angel roared, a sound of pain, "His life is mine!", he screamed again But nature's force, could not be swayed, The boy's short time, had been displayed.

He knew he had to make a choice, To let fate win, and silence voice. Or make his own change, and break the chain, And fight for love, and life again. He pushed with all, his might and soul, To

give the boy a life to extol. And with
one last push, the branch let go, The
angel collapsed, with head hung low.
The boy was safe, beneath the shade,
The angel fought, the choice was made
He looked at him, the small boy there,
And in his eyes, a love so rare, The
angel smiled, with bittersweet grace,
And knew he couldn't leave this place.

The boy he ran, with open arms, "You
saved me!" and with all his charms He
hugged the man, and thanked him true,
And whispered "I love you". The angel's
heart, no longer torn, A second chance,
a new life born. He knew where destiny
should roam, He'd find this boy, and
make a home. He'd teach him love, and
warmth and joy, And be his father, to
this small boy. And though his task,
was left undone, He knew his life, had
just begun. The boy he stayed, and then
he grew, With the angel, kind and true.
No longer orphan, lost and lone, He
found the love, he'd always known. And
though the tree, still stands in place,
They found their joy, and loving space.
Because this angel, took a stand, And
changed the boy's fate, with his hand.

11. A WALK IN THE COLD HILLS

The city's hum, a cage I'd built of
steel, Had choked the life from what I
used to feel. The weight of deals, the
boardroom's sterile glare, Had left me
hollow, lost in deep despair. So I fled,
a CEO uncrowned, From Bangalore's grasp,
to where peace was found. Wellington's
hills, a verdant, sloping grace,
Pemberly's tea estates, a tranquil
space.

A hamlet nestled, small and quaint and
still, Became my refuge, on a lonely
hill. I sat upon a fence, of weathered
wood, And watched the world, as only
drifters could. An old woman, bent with
years and toil, Was gathering wood,
upon this fertile soil. The forest
whispered secrets, soft and low, As she
bound the branches, in a weary show.

She struggled with the bundle, twice it
fell, Then turned her gaze, where I my
vigil held. A calloused hand, she waved,
a plea to see, And beckoned me, to walk
towards her, free. With strength I'd
long ignored, I raised the load, And
placed it firmly, on her frail abode.
She thanked me with a smile, both warm
and deep, And spoke of solitude,
secrets she would keep.

She shared her tale, of life within
these hills, Of lonely days, and time
that slowly spills. Her son, she said,

had sought the city's hum, Sent money
once, then silence, cruel and numb. A
widow's pension, barely kept her fed, A
life of poverty, in shadows bred. She
walked ahead, I followed in her wake,
Towards a mud hut, for my soul's own
sake.

Her humble dwelling, with its earthen
floor, Offered me a seat, a wooden box,
and more. Lukewarm water, in a chipped,
old cup, I drank with thirsty haste,
then lifted up My head to see, a
photograph so clear, A young man's face,
it struck a chord of fear. A driver's
face, I knew it all too well, Whose
life was lost, the day my car did fell.

His eyes, so full of life, now looked
at me, Accusing, from beyond the veil I
see. My guilt, a tidal wave, descended
slow, The car crash's horror, back in
painful flow. I'd fled my life, to find
some inner peace, But God had sent me
here, for soul's release. This woman's
son, the man who drove my car, And now,
I saw, what penance I must bear.

I shed my coat, of city's rigid mold,
And took the axe, its handle strong and
bold. The wood piled high before me, my
task clear, To serve this woman,
conquer every fear. The cold air bit,
but warmth began to bloom, As I worked
with purpose, chasing off the gloom.
Each swing of steel, a prayer, each
splintered piece, A fragile hope of
finding inner peace.

Rehana, Zubaidha and other poor souls...

The scent of wood, and sweat upon my
brow, A purpose found, I knew it here
and now. The weight of deals, the
city's hurried pace, Were fading fast,
in this secluded space. No longer CEO,
but simple, strong and free, I chopped
the wood for her, for him, for me. The
old woman watched, with gentle, tearful
eyes, As I began to build, beneath the
mountain skies.

The loneliness she knew, now shared
with me, A burden lifted, now our souls
felt free. The city's clamor, a distant,
fading sound, As in this hamlet, true
solace could be found. With each stroke
of the axe, a step I took, Towards
redemption, from the lies I'd cooked. I
came to hide, but God had other plans,
To heal my heart, with calloused,
working hands.

This walk in the hills, in the cold's
embrace, Revealed the truth, of time
and love and space. And though the road
is long, and trials deep, In serving
others, my soul finds sleep. So let the
city's giants, greedily amass, I'll
stay here rooted, where true values
last. With axe in hand, and heart so
full of grace, I'll face my penance, in
this quiet place. And maybe then, the
son will know my deed, And find his
peace, for he's the one I need, To
forgive my fault, my callous act, And
finally understand, time can never go
back.

12. THE LANTERN OF LOST LOVE

A tale it is, of salt and stone, where waves do carve their cruel design, Of Carolina, newly wed, her heart a fragile, trembling shrine. The statue stands, a silent guide, a lady carved in weathered grey, Her lantern held, a watchful eye, upon the restless, churning bay. Just like she, Carolina waits, though storm clouds gather, dark and deep, Her own small lantern, amber bright, a vigil she's resolved to keep.

The thatched roof hut, now left untended, the warmth within now cold and bare, She walks the path, each step a prayer, upon the wind, a whispered care. Her neighborhood aunts, with eyes of knowing, their warnings echoed in the breeze, "The sea, my child, she holds no mercy, she takes what pleases, as she please." But Carolina, headstrong, young, her love a wild and burning fire, Ignores their pleas, their worried clucking, fueled by an ardent, deep desire.

Yesterday, the church bells pealed, a promise sealed with sacred vow, St. Francis' ancient walls did witness, the vows they spoke, and took somehow. A simple band, upon her finger, a circle binding heart to soul, A memory of Thomas's warm smile, before the sea did claim its toll. He left at dawn, while stars still lingered, for depths unknown, his boat did glide, A promise whispered, a new home built, with love as his most trusted guide.

A stone house, strong, for her protection, a promise made with tender grace, He'd brave the waves, though shadows threatened, to build her love a fitting space. The weather forecast, a whispered warning, of fury brewing, black and vast, The other boats, all safely anchored, their captains wise, the die was cast. But Thomas sailed, his heart was driven, by love and hope, a burning need, To fulfill his promise, and her wishes, a loving heart, a noble deed.

Now twilight falls, a bruised embrace, the orange sun descends from sight, No single sail upon the horizon, only darkness, and coming night. She scans the waves, her eyes are pleading, seeking a mast, a familiar form, The sea a canvas, dark and empty, swallowed by the brewing storm. The lighthouse beacon, a sweeping searchlight, cuts through the gloom, a lonely call, But only answers with the echo, of waves that rise, and then they fall.

She kneels upon the cold, wet sand, her fingers trace the wedding ring, A silent plea, a heartfelt prayer, to the heavens, help him to bring. Memories flicker, like the lantern, of Thomas's touch, his gentle hold, The warmth he brought, the love he shared, a story now, yet to unfold. She remembers

kisses, whispered nothings, promises
beneath the moonlit sky, He'd held her
close, and promised her forever, now,
just the waves, they softly cry.

The tide, it creeps, with hungry
fingers, it laps at shore, with cruel
delight, An angry mistress, claiming
victims, in the dark of the approaching
night. The wind picks up, it howls and
whispers, tales of sailors lost at sea,
And Carolina, she trembles, fear it
takes, a hold now, she cannot flee. Did
he feel the cold, the ocean's grip? Did
he call her name, in his despair? Were
his last thoughts of her, she wonders?
Lost in the ocean's cold, grey lair.

The lantern light begins to flicker,
its fragile flame, a wavering glow,
Reflecting in her tear-filled eyes,
where fear and grief begin to grow. She
watches, waits, with unwavering faith,
her heart a fragile, wounded thing,
Praying for a miracle to happen, for
love's return, on hopeful wing. But the
sea, she is unyielding, she offers no
comfort, no release, Only the endless,
crashing waves, a symphony of no inner
peace.

The hours pass, like restless spirits,
the night is long, the darkness reigns,
And Carolina, she refuses, to let go,
of her heart's refrains. She sees the
form of the stone lady, her lantern's
beam, a silent plea, Reflecting her own
unwavering vigil, beside the boundless,

cruel sea. A bond of sadness, yet of
solace, a shared existence, etched in
stone, Two ladies waiting, for lost
loved hearts, each on the shore,
utterly alone.

The morning breaks, a pale and fragile
light, it crawls across the eastern sky,
But Thomas's boat, still absent,
nowhere to be seen, just the gulls cry.
The tide has turned, its anger waning,
a stillness claims the restless space,
But in her heart, the storm still rages,
a wound that time will not erase. The
fisherfolk, they gather near her, their
faces etched with silent woe, They knew
the sea, her cruel intentions, the
bitter truth, they all did know.

And Carolina, stood there, on the shore,
amidst the sun's pale, morning rays,
She knew that Thomas wouldn't return,
and their love, just a memory always.
Her lantern dims, its flame
extinguished, as the sun begins its
gentle climb, A symbol of her fading
hope, lost in the relentless march of
time. But in the tales, of the village
people, of love and loss, the story
stays, Of Carolina, and the stone
statue, and their lanterns, through the
ocean's haze.

The lady with the lantern, a new story
told, now had a partner in grief and
despair, Carolina, the heartbroken wife,
whose love remained, beyond compare.
And though the waves still crash and

thunder, their mournful song will forever say, Of love's pure light, forever burning, even when hope has sailed away. For in each lantern's flicker, we see, a testament to love's great might, A beacon shining, in the darkness, a promise kept, both day and night. The sea may claim, and take, and borrow, but love remains, an endless tide, And Carolina's vigil continues, where true love, forever does abide.

13. PANCHAKALYANI'S LAMENT

A wild heart, a storm in hoof and mane,
They called me Panchakalyani, a spirit
untamed, In Delhi's dust, where empires
rose and fell, I stood defiant, a
legend to compel.

No rider's hand, no bit, no cruel
design, Could bend my will, this
strength that was all mine. Then came
the Sultan, with a twisted, cunning
game: "Tame the beast," he roared, "and
win back freedom's flame!"

Kings and princes, they came like moths
to fire, Their fragile hands, their
hopes, their futile desire. One by one,
they fell, their pride in chains
confined, In the Sultan's dungeons,
their freedom left behind.

Swaroop Singh of Senji, the East's
proud Troy, Met the same fate, his
spirit, a broken toy. But from his
lineage, a son, a burning light, Young
Desingh Raja, came to claim his right.

A wild young man, with shoulders built
like stone, He faced the Sultan, his
challenge bravely sown. "Tame the
beast," they cried, "or join your
father's plight," I pawed the earth, a
challenge, dark and bright.

Rehana, Zubaidha and other poor souls...

The day arrived, I felt the ground
beneath me heave, The Sultan's gaze, a
judgment to conceive. I ran in circles,
a tempest unbound, His frantic efforts,
falling to the ground.

He chased and lunged, I mocked his
flailing hand, Another king, I thought,
soon to be outmanned. But something
shifted, in his eyes, a burning gleam,
He rose each time, with strength, it
would seem.

He failed and failed, yet came again
anew, His determination, fiercely
shining through. He lunged and grasped,
his grip like iron chains, My will gave
way, I felt the pull, the strain.

My spirit yielded, a battle fought and
lost, Beneath his weight, a surrender,
at great cost. He rode me then, before
the crowd's acclaim, The Sultan paled,
defeated in his game.

Desingh was hailed, Raja of Senji
proclaimed, The kings were freed, their
freedom now reclaimed, But my new rider,
had other plans it seemed, He claimed
me as his prize, a vision I had dreamed.

Away from Delhi, to Senji we now flew,
Past plains and rivers, my journey,
fresh and new. My king, he never
whipped, nor cursed in vain, He rode
with passion, freedom, and the rain.

Senji welcomed, me with open arms, And
I was treated, freed from all harms No
stable walls, for me, only love and
care, He took me everywhere, no burden
to bear.

To temples grand, and hillsides cool
and high, I knew his kingdom, beneath
the vast blue sky. This land of plenty,
where the rivers flowed so free, I was
happy now, safe from the wicked decree.

But alas, a shadow from the past took
form, Yusuf Khan, the traitor, brewing
up a storm. Expelled from Senji, for
his vile, cruel deeds, He sought
revenge, sowing Arcot's wicked seeds.

He stole the parchment, Delhi's gift,
it's claim, And demanded tax, in Arcot
Nawaab's name. Desingh stood firm, his
refusal, proud and bold, Then Arcot
struck, a story to be told.

War came like thunder, unexpected,
fierce and fast, My king's friend,
Mohammed Khan, his marriage overcast.
The wedding stopped, he donned his
armour bright, And stood beside Desingh,
ready for the fight.

Across the Pennar, they held the enemy
at bay, But victory faltered, on that
tragic day. Mohammed Khan fell, his
life cut short and brief, A hero's
sacrifice, a nation felt the grief.

The enemy pressed, the river swollen
high, I felt a burning pain, a wound I
could not deny, A sword had struck me,
the enemy's cruel blow, But I kept
moving, my king I would not let go.

We turned towards the fort, a desperate
fight, But the bridge was ablaze, a
horrifying sight. We leapt into the
river, a perilous way, To reach the
other side, before the end of day.

The current surged, the rocks were
sharp and cold, I struggled on, my
strength was growing old. The wound, it
spread, a burning, icy pain, My legs
gave out, my strength, no more to gain.

I stumbled, shuddered, my body went so
cold, I threw my king to the shore, my
story to unfold. I failed my king, my
purpose left undone, I saw the enemies,
surrounding him as the setting sun.

My eyes grew dim, the world began to
fade, I, Panchakalyani, in this river's
bed was laid. My heart, it broke, with
sorrow, pain, and dread, I failed my
king, and my spirit slowly fled.

14. THE KEEPER'S SON

A thatched roof, hunched and low, it
stood, Where earth met sky,
misunderstood, A corner of the
graveyard's gray domain, Where life's
brief candle flickered, dim, in vain.
Young Johny knew no other home, no
other sight, Than weathered stones and
shadows of the night. His father,
Abraham, a keeper of this place, Now
rested there, beneath the cold earth's
face.

His mother, Mary, lean and worn and
slight, Clung to the graveyard's edge
with all her might. Her world, a circle,
etched in grief's own hand, Her
husband's grave, a sacred, silent
strand. She would not leave, though
whispered pleas arose From village folk,
who pitied her, God knows. A mile away,
where laughter danced and played, The
village children, in the sunbeam swayed.

But Johny, eight years old, with
boundless heart, Yearned for that world,
to play a different part. He longed for
games, for friends, for open spaces,
Not graves that cast their shadows on
his faces. He'd wake in dread, from
nightmares, faces blurred, Of ghostly
figures, from the earth uncurled. His
schoolmates mocked, "The graveyard
boy," they'd sneer, And fear of spirits
filled his heart with fear.

Each day, he'd beg his mother, restless, tired, "The village church, the market," he desired. "Let's fish beyond the cliffs," his constant plea, To leave the headstones, finally to be free. He'd carry rod and hook, the worm-filled tin, A boy escaping, from the shadows within. The graveyard loomed, a constant, chilling weight, A place of fear that sealed his fragile fate.

The church's dole, a meager, humble thing, Barely enough to make their spirits sing. For clothes were worn, and toys were distant dreams, Just food enough, to quell life's raging streams. Mary, when the catch was good, divided what she caught One day for them, the rest she gave, unsought. She never went to mass, her clothes too bare, But Johny went, a silent, lonely prayer.

She, in her late twenties, looked much older grown, By hard work and despair, her spirit prone. The church had urged, "The boy, an orphan's life," "Let us provide, from care and endless strife." "And you with us, you'll find a worthy place," "In seminary kitchens, filled with grace." Yet Mary's heart, it held a stubborn sway, Her husband's grave, she'd never turn away.

One evening, by the hut, the fire burned low, She cooked their meal, her thoughts began to flow. Of Abraham's smile, his touch, his loving gaze, A

life now lost, in time's forgotten maze.
She yearned, she wished, for life
beyond the stones, A life in the
village, free from weary moans. A
sudden heat, a flicker, then a flame,
Her dress ignited, a terrifying game.

She screamed, and fell, upon the dusty
floor, A neighbor rushed, but knew it
was no more, The damage done, a life
too quickly burned, Her last breath
given, fate's cruel lesson learned.
They came for Johny, a vision veiled in
cloth, No gentle face, just grief, and
bitter wrath, They took her body, and
in the ground she lay, Beside her
husband, as her soul did stray.

Johny lay there, through the long and
lonely night Upon the wet earth, where
she lost the light. The graveyard, once
a haunting, dreaded place, Became a
haven now, for grief's cold embrace.
His mother lay there, silent and at
rest. How could he leave her here, and
face the test, Of village life, with
laughter, joy, and play, When she was
here, where shadows held their sway?

He stayed, he watched, beside his
mother's mound, The graveyard's son, in
sorrow deeply bound. The hut remained,
his shelter and his keep, And in the
quiet graves, did memories sleep. No
longer fear, he felt a mournful peace,
Among the headstones, knew his soul's
release The boy who yearned to leave,
his heart now bound, To silent stones,

Rehana, Zubaidha and other poor souls...

where love was always found The
Keeper's son, forever now to stay,
Beside the graveyard, come what may.

15. THE REAL HEAVEN

The salt-laced wind, a constant,
mournful sigh, Whispered tales of
Bijlee, beneath the sky.

A fisherman he was, his hands, sun-
kissed and worn,
Now sought the sea's vast heart, a
sailor newly born.

His village hugged the shore, a cluster
small and tight,
Where children's laughter echoed, both
morning, noon and night.

Their tiny hands, so eager, would tug
his nets with glee,
And his small boat, their playground, a
constant misery.

They'd tangle ropes, and splinter wood,
with shouts of pure delight,
While Bijlee, patience waning, would
chase them from his sight.

He'd curse their playful chaos, and the
market's fishy reek,
And dreamed of quiet oceans, a solace
he would seek.

Loneliness, a constant ache, a hollow
in his soul, Spurred him to seek
adventure, beyond the tidal shoal.

He bought a small white yacht, with
sails that yearned to fly,

And set his course to southward,
beneath the endless sky.

Into the Indian Ocean, he ventured,
brave and bold,
Leaving behind the village, its stories
to be told.

The waves grew high and angry, the sky
turned inky black,
A fearsome storm descended, upon his
fragile track.

The yacht was tossed and battered, its
mast a cracking sound,
While Bijlee fought the tempest, with
courage tightly bound.
He tied himself with rope, to keep from
being swept
Into the churning water, where the
ship's breath sadly wept.

He struggled, swam, and fought to reach
the boat,
The storm, relentless, mocking his
strained float.

The waves swallowed him whole, beneath
the raging might,
And in the endless darkness, he
surrendered to the night.

Then came a gentle chirping, a sound
both sweet and clear,
As if a tiny angel chased away his fear.

He woke to whitest sand, kissed by a
gentle breeze,

A shore unknown, untainted, beneath the
emerald trees.

No village, no fish market, no
children's noisy plays,
Just a silent, sun-kissed cove, in a
world of warmer rays.
An island, strangely wondrous, with
flowers bold and bright,
And meadows, emerald carpets, bathed in
a soft, warm light.

Fruit trees of every color, a bounty
he'd not known,
Hung heavy with their sweetness, a
feast for him alone.

No broken jetty, scorching heat, no
earthly, harsh despair,
Just quiet, soothing silence, and a
sweet, scented air.

He sang with newfound freedom, as he
walked through that strange place,
No longer burdened by the world, a
smile upon his face

He built a small stone shelter, beneath
the fragrant trees,
And savored every moment, of this newfound liberties.

He ate his fill of fruits, sweet, juicy
and unknown,
And lay each night in peace, finally,
he was alone.

One day, a figure tall arose, amidst
the fruit trees there,

A man of noble bearing, planting a tree
with care.

He watched him, strong and vibrant,
watering the soil,
And followed him, intending, to share
his newfound toil.

But when he spoke, the figure vanished
in the wood,
Leaving Bijlee puzzled, misunderstood.

The very next dawn, the figure was
mowing the meadows grand,
With a large mower, moving in a swift,
steady hand.

Once again Bijlee approached him, to
break the lonely chain
But once again he disappeared, like a
ghost in the rain.

The next day, Bijlee waited, by the
forest's shadowed edge,
But the figure never appeared, no hint
of any ledge.

He waited and he watched, for days that
turned to weeks,
Hoping just to glimpse him, if only
some quick streaks.

Then one dawn, upon the hill, the
figure stood in sight,
Looking down at the bay, bathed in the
morning light.

Bijlee ran to catch him, and touched
his back with care,

And asked, with quiet wonder, "Who are
you, standing there?"

The man turned, with eyes of wisdom,
and spoke in gentle tone,
"My name is not your concern," he said,
"You are not alone.

You were not disturbed, and i never
disturbed you so why are you
questioning me now?"
his thoughts began to flow.

Bijlee persisted, "Why are you here on
this new ground?"
The man's reply was simple, without a
trace of sound.

"I plant these trees and mow the
grass," he said, with a gentle smile,
"So you can live in peace, and rest for
a long, long while."

 Bijlee, confused, then asked, "But why
would you do this for me?
" The man said, "For you, Bijlee, I
made it all to be.

You yearned for a place of solace,
where sadness cannot grow,
A piece of paradise, Bijlee, where your
soul could truly flow.

You wanted a place to be, with no one
to disturb, So, I created this haven,
and never left you curb".

Bijlee looked at him, eyes wide, with
understanding deep,

Realized the man before him, made the
mountains weep.

This was no mortal presence, but
something more divine,
"Are you God?" Bijlee whispered, "Is
this heavenly shrine?"

"It is," the man responded, "This place
you have found so fair,
Is Paradise, it's heaven, free from all
earthly care.

" And then he simply vanished, into the
soft bright haze,
Leaving Bijlee pondering, in a peaceful,
silent state.

He never felt the hunger, no sweat upon
his brow,
He built his home with ease, no
feelings of pain now.

He walked and sang with joy, the fruits
sustained his soul,
He confirmed this was heaven, a life
completely whole.

But days turned into months, and the
silence started deep,
A new ache settled in, as he drifted
off to sleep.

He longed for earth's familiar hum, the
children, the market sound,
He missed the broken jetty, where chaos
did abound.

He walked along the shoreline, endless
and so grand,
His heaven, now a gilded cage, within
this lonely land.

A sadness overwhelmed him, his strength
began to wane,
He fainted on the shore there, calling
out for rain.

Then voices, soft and distant, broke
the silent spell,
  "Hey, it's Bijlee, come help lift him,
are you going well?

" He felt hands beneath him, strong and
rough and kind,
And heard his name repeated, as he left
paradise behind.
He opened weary eyelids, to see
familiar faces, His neighbors, his
village folks, in their known familiar
spaces.

The children, shouting happily, "Bijlee
is awake!
" His heart filled with a longing, that
heaven just could not break.

He was back in his village, his hut,
his simple life,
He'd traveled to a paradise, escaping
all the strife,

But paradise was lonely, a place to be
alone,
He saw in those dear faces, a truth
that had been shown.

This was his true heaven, with
neighbors, children, friends,
A place where someone's helping hands,
his need attends.

The chaos, and the noise, the fish
market's pungent smell,
Were pieces of his heaven, his story
they all tell.

For true heaven, Bijlee realized, is
not a place apart,
But in the love and laughter, living in
each heart.
He smiled, and rose up, thankful, for
his life's chaotic art,
And knew, finally, he had come home, to
the heaven of his heart.

16. FORGIVENESS

The salt spray stung my face as the ferry churned through the choppy waters, each thrust a mocking echo of the turmoil in my heart. Rangat Island, a speck of green in the vast blue, was my destination, or rather, the end of my road. I, Bala, a thirty-four-year-old man drowning in a sea of my own making, was running away, not to something, but from everything.

Swapna, my wife, the woman two years my senior, the one I had secretly married seven years ago, had ripped open the carefully constructed façade of my life. The dirty secret was out. My parents, my colleagues, everyone knew. And the shame, the utter humiliation, it was a crushing weight. Swapna, divorced before me, had done it deliberately. The fight, the accusations, the recriminations... I couldn't bear it anymore. My life, a carefully balanced act, had collapsed. Suicide was the only solution. And Rangat, far from the judging eyes of Port Blair, was to be my final stage.

The island welcomed me with the scent of damp earth and unfamiliar birdsong. I walked aimlessly, the jungle a claustrophobic embrace. Reaching the edge of a small village, I saw a stream gurgling over smooth stones, and on the other side, nestled at the foot of a small hill, was a hut. Smoke curled lazily from its chimney, and a small, whitewashed temple stood serenely beside the stream. Drawn by an unseen force, I crossed the water on stepping-stones.

An old man sat outside the hut, his face a roadmap of wrinkles, his eyes like ancient pools reflecting untold stories. He looked at me, and a chill ran down my spine. He didn't ask my name or where I was from, instead, he said, "You come here burdened by a secret, a marriage hidden like a dark stain. You carry the weight of your parents' disappointment, the whispers of colleagues, and the betrayal by the woman you chose. You seek escape, but the problem is not in the world outside but in the chambers of your own heart, my son."

Every word felt like a hammer blow. I stared at him, aghast. How could he possibly know? I hadn't spoken to a soul. Yet, his gaze held no malice, only a profound understanding. He didn't offer me false comfort or empty platitudes. Instead, he spoke of choices, of consequences, of the pain we inflict upon ourselves. He spoke of the folly of running away and the courage required to face our imperfections and right the wrong. I sat there for hours, listening, the old man's voice a balm on my wounded soul. He didn't offer solutions, but he made me see my own problems, starkly and clearly.

The next day, I wandered to the other side of the island, drawn by some unknown impulse. There, on a small hillock, overlooking the vast ocean, was another humble hut. A woman, seemingly as ancient as the hills, with eyes that twinkled like distant stars, greeted me. Her smile was warm, and she invited me to sit. I wasn't surprised when she also, without any preamble, started talking about my past, about the hidden marriage, about the shame and despair I was carrying.

"My son," she said, her voice like the gentle sigh of the wind, "you are not running from your problems; you are running from yourself. The river cannot return to its source, but the pain can be washed clean. Your parents, they are like aged trees, deeply rooted in love. They may be hurt, but the core of their being is forgiveness. They will be waiting with an open heart, waiting just to see you. Go back to them, my child, and make amends. It is not weakness; it is true strength."

Her words resonated with a truth that shook me to my core. I had been so consumed by my own self-pity, I hadn't considered the pain I had inflicted on my parents. The old woman advised me, "Life is not about running away, my son. It's about facing your mistakes and learning from them." An odd sense of calm washed over me.

The three-day ship journey to Chennai felt like a lifetime. I was a changed man, or at least, a man in the process of change. I was no longer running from my life, however messed up it had become. I was running towards a resolve.

Arriving in Chennai, the city's cacophony was a stark contrast to the serene quietude of Rangat. Instead of booking a ticket back home, I took a bus to Krishnagiri. My dark thoughts returned, a cruel reminder of my earlier desire to end it all. The Krishnagiri hills were known to be a haven for those with despair in their hearts. I started to climb, the rocky path mirroring the steep climb of my past mistakes.

Halfway up, I saw a dargah, a Muslim shrine, nestled amidst the rocks. A moment of surprise hit me as that was the last thing I expected. I walked past, half-heartedly, thinking it would be the place where I would end myself, some peace in the midst of the religious shrine. I had almost reached the other side when a voice stopped me. "Young man," it called.

An old Mulla with a flowing white beard and kind eyes beckoned me closer. He didn't know me, but just like on the islands, he knew everything about me. "Son," he said, "your worries are over. The mountains behind you are not for endings. Your parents' home is the true path for you. Return to them; you will find peace there."

I stood there, completely stunned. Three times, in three different places, I had been met with the same message. Was the Universe speaking to me? Was it a sign? Whatever it was, it changed me. I descended the hills, a renewed purpose flowing through my veins. I booked a bus ticket to my hometown, 300 kilometers away.

The final bus journey was a blur of emotions. Fear, anticipation, and a strange sense of hope warred within me. My parents' house loomed before me, a beacon of familiarity in my chaotic life. The door creaked open, and my mother stood there, her eyes filled with tears. I had expected anger, recriminations, but all I saw was a profound love. My father emerged from the shadows, his face etched with worry, but his hand reached out to me.

There were no harsh words, only tears and embraces. They had known all along, they told me. They had always loved me, they could not be angry at their own son. We talked for hours that night, the years of silence broken by a flood of confessions and forgiveness. It wasn't a fairytale ending. There were still wounds to heal, but it was a beginning. A beginning built on acceptance and love and the courage to face the mistakes of my past. I had finally stopped running and came home, not behind the hills, but to my parents.

17. **THE WHISPERS OF AVADI**

The sun, a molten coin in the morning sky, would always find its way through the dense foliage that encircled the four houses. This was Avadi, a town on the outskirts of Chennai, where paddy fields stretched like emerald carpets and a serpentine river whispered secrets to the lake nearby. Within this verdant embrace, lived Balaji and his sprawling family - a microcosm of life, love, and the enduring ache of the human heart.

Balaji's childhood was a vibrant tapestry woven with the threads of twenty lives. His house, one of four in the compound, was always alive with the clamor of his elder sister Chitra, the playful antics of his younger sister Priya, and the comforting presence of his parents. Grandparents, uncles, aunts, and their numerous children completed the boisterous ensemble. The air buzzed with laughter, the clatter of plates, and the comforting hum of familial bonds. Balaji, a boy with eyes as soft as the paddy fields and a heart as gentle as the river's flow, thrived in this environment. He was the peacemaker, the helping hand, the embodiment of quiet kindness.

But even in this lively microcosm, a different kind of stirring began in young Balaji. Across the hedge, in the neighboring house, lived the parents and their four daughters. Among them was Sharmila. At the tender age of seven, Sharmila, with her eyes that mirrored the dark waters of the lake and a smile that could charm the birds from the trees, captured Balaji's heart. His innocent admiration blossomed into something deeper as the years spun by.

He watched her from afar, his young heart brimming with a love he couldn't yet articulate. The passing years morphed into a decade. Balaji, now a young man in his teens, finally found the courage to speak. It was a confession delivered with trepidation, a heart laid bare. Sharmila, caught off-guard, initially rejected him. Her "no" echoed through the space between their houses, a chilling counterpoint to the warmth he had always felt. But Balaji, with the resilience of a sapling bending in the wind, didn't give up. He continued to express his love and waited.

A year later, her heart swayed, and she cautiously accepted.

Their young love unfolded in secret whispers under the mango trees, stolen glances across the hedge, and fleeting touches. It was a tender love, fragile and beautiful. But life, as it always does, had its cruel twists to deliver. A tragedy descended upon Balaji's family when his sister Chitra succumbed to a sudden illness. The grief was profound, a wound that cut deep into the very core of their being. The family, in a haze of sorrow, decided to move, their roots uprooted and replanted twenty miles away.

Balaji carried Sharmila's heart with him, a precious relic of his simpler, happier days. But distance worked its insidious magic. Sharmila's affections started to cool. The flame that had kindled between them faded, leaving behind the cold ashes of heartbreak. She abandoned him, her feelings a fleeting whisper rather than the enduring love he had hoped for. She married another man, leaving Balaji shattered, the pieces of his heart scattered like autumn leaves.

The silence that followed was deafening. For two years, Balaji retreated into himself, the laughter of his childhood replaced by a quiet anguish. He became a ghost in his own life until a woman, older than him by two years, entered. Swapna was a divorced woman, her eyes holding the wisdom of a life lived and some battles fought. She saw past Balaji's silence, sensing the depth of his pain. She slowly coaxed him back to the world, her kindness a balm to his wounded soul. He fell in love with her but she being a divorced woman, was met with disapproval from his parents. This led them to choose to marry secretly. They took their vows and became husband and wife, a union that they hoped would last forever.

With Swapna, Balaji found a different kind of love – mature, passionate, and comforting. He threw his full support to her. He encouraged her, supporting her through tough exams and training so she could pursue a civil engineering degree. He made her an engineer, her own pride. He then secured a government job in the Andaman Islands, an archipelago far from the familiar landscapes of Avadi. He took Swapna with him, hoping for a new beginning.

But in Port Blair, a different storm was brewing. Swapna, burdened by the ghosts of her past, carried a deep insecurity. She had undergone a tubectomy after having two children whom she left with her ex-husband, and the fact that she couldn't give him children fueled her fears. She lived in constant suspicion, convinced that Balaji would eventually abandon her for a woman who could fulfill his family's desire for an heir. She became possessive, controlling his every interaction, forbidding him from speaking to other women, even in jest. Her paranoia grew, casting a long shadow over their lives.

The weight of her suspicion became unbearable, eroding their love like the ceaseless tide. At the age of 60 she opened up about their marriage to Balaji's superiors and the family. The burden of secrecy and Swapna's constant accusations became too great for Balaji. His shame was a heavy cloak of defeat. In a moment of despair, he sought solace on a remote island, contemplating the ultimate escape. But something within him shifted. He turned back, his heart heavy, the realization of his worth now apparent, the desire to live again now surging.

He returned home, told his parents everything, and made the difficult decision to divorce Swapna. He chose to live life according to his own choices and not by the choices of others. And with the divorce finalized, he began to feel freedom and peace. He chose to return to Port Blair, to live a lonely but peaceful life, a life without the chains of despair. He accepted his life, embracing the solitude. He worked in his office during the day and returned home in the evenings. He cooked for himself and relaxed with some music. He was happy with the peace and calm. He began to wait with hope for someone who would love him for who he is. He awaited a best life partner.

Balaji's story is not one of grand triumphs or spectacular failures but a testament to the quiet strength of the human heart. It is a story of a boy who loved deeply, lost painfully, and learned to navigate the complexities of life with grace and resilience. The whispers of Avadi still echoes in his memories, a reminder of the love he once knew and the journey he continues to traverse.

18. THE LUNAR WHISPER – PART ONE

The sterile white walls of the Roscosmos training facility buzzed with a nervous energy. Five figures, silhouettes against the harsh fluorescent lights, were about to embark on a journey unlike any other. Their destination: the Lunar Power Station, the pulsating heart of Earth's energy grid, built within the shadowed craters of the Moon, without which the entire earth would be in darkness. Their mission: to keep it running. Their odds: less than encouraging.

Among them was Dr. Natalia Sharma, a woman of Indian origin with a fierce intellect and an unwavering determination etched onto her face. She was surrounded by her Russian crewmates: Commander Dimitri Volkov, a veteran cosmonaut with a stoic demeanor; Anya Petrova, a brilliant engineer with haunted eyes; Boris Ivanov, a burly geologist whose jovial nature masked a deep-seated fear; and Sergei Morozov, a quiet astrophysicist known for his meticulous calculations.

The Lunar Power Station was a marvel, a testament to human ingenuity and a symbol of global cooperation. A massive complex powered by lunar-mined uranium, it beamed clean, sustainable energy back to Earth, a solution to the planet's energy crisis. But the station held a dark secret, a terrifying whisper that echoed in the sterile halls of mission control.

Every year, a team of five individuals was sent to maintain the station for ten days. The six superpowers – Russia, China, the United States, the European Union, India, and Japan – took turns. But the return rate was abysmal. Only two or three usually made it back, and those survivors were invariably afflicted with severe memory loss, their minds fractured, their stories fragmented.

Natalia knew the statistics. She had pored over the reports, analyzed the data, searched for patterns. But the answers remained elusive, shrouded in the cold, unyielding vacuum of space and the insidious effects of the lunar environment.

She had one week before launch, one week to unravel the mystery that clung to the Lunar Power Station like lunar dust. And the key, she believed, lay with someone who had faced the station's horrors and lived to tell the tale – or at least, a portion of it.

Her target: Dr. Wu Shin, a renowned Chinese physicist and the sole survivor of the Chinese team sent to the station two years prior. He had returned a broken man, his brilliant mind riddled with gaps, his memories fragmented into unsettling images and whispered phrases. The Chinese government had shielded him from outside contact, deeming him too unstable for public interaction.

But Natalia was not easily deterred. She knew this was a long shot, a gamble against time and political walls. With her Roscosmos credentials and a carefully constructed narrative about sharing research data, she managed to secure a visa to China.

The bustling streets of Shanghai felt alien after the cold precision of the Roscosmos facility. She found Dr. Wu Shin in a secluded sanatorium nestled in the hills outside the city. The facility was discreet, its purpose masked behind manicured gardens and a facade of tranquility.

Dr. Wu Shin was a shadow of his former self. His eyes, once bright with scientific curiosity, were now clouded with confusion and fear. He sat in a dimly lit room, meticulously arranging pebbles on the floor, his movements slow and deliberate.

Natalia managed to disguise as a nurse and crossed all the securities and finally approached him cautiously, in a hushed voice speaking in Mandarin, a language she had painstakingly learned for this very encounter. "Dr. Wu Shin, my name is Dr. Natalia Sharma. I am with the Russian space program."

He didn't react, his gaze fixed on the pebbles.

"I am going to the Lunar Power Station," Natalia continued, her voice gentle. "I need your help. I need to understand what happened to you there."

His hand froze mid-air. He slowly turned his head, his eyes finally focusing on her. A flicker of recognition, or perhaps fear, flashed across his face.

"The whispers," he rasped, his voice barely audible. "They never stop."

Natalia leaned closer. "What whispers, Dr. Wu Shin? What are you talking about?"

He began to tremble, his body wracked with shivers. "The moon... it speaks. It doesn't want us there. It punishes those who listen."

Natalia pressed him further, asking about the accidents, the equipment malfunctions, the strange occurrences that had plagued previous missions. But his answers were fragmented, disjointed, laced with paranoia. He spoke of shadows moving in the periphery of vision, of sounds that defied explanation, of a growing sense of unease that permeated the entire station.
He remembered a power surge, a sudden spike in radiation levels, followed by a wave of nausea and disorientation. He remembered his crewmates acting strangely, their personalities shifting, their words

becoming nonsensical. And he remembered the whispers, the voices that seemed to emanate from the very fabric of the moon, whispering secrets, whispering madness.
He claimed that the lunar uranium wasn't just fueling the station, it was amplifying something, something ancient and malevolent that resided on the moon. The station was not just a power source, it was a conduit, a gateway.

"They are draining our memories," he said, his voice rising in a panic. "They are taking our souls. We are becoming…empty."

His words were unsettling, bordering on delusional. But Natalia couldn't dismiss them entirely. There was a raw terror in his eyes, a genuine belief in what he was saying.

Natalia spent the next few days with Dr. Wu Shin, patiently piecing together his fragmented memories. She learned about strange symbols etched into the lunar rock near the mining site, symbols that resembled nothing she had ever seen. She learned about a hidden chamber within the station, a place forbidden to all but a select few individuals.

And she learned about a recurring nightmare that haunted him: a vision of the Earth, slowly turning black, dying as the Lunar Power Station silently pulsed with an unnatural energy.

Natalia left China with more questions than answers. Dr. Wu Shin's testimony was unreliable, tainted by trauma and potential mental instability. But she also couldn't shake the feeling that there was a kernel of truth hidden within his ramblings, a truth that could hold the key to understanding the mysteries of the Lunar Power Station.

Back in Russia, Natalia shared her findings with Commander Volkov, the mission leader. He listened patiently, his face betraying nothing. When she finished, he simply nodded.
"Dr. Sharma," he said, his voice calm and measured. "We are soldiers. We follow orders. Our mission is to maintain the Lunar Power Station, regardless of the risks."

Natalia knew that arguing was futile. The mission was already set in motion, the political and economic stakes too high to back down. But she was determined to uncover the truth, even if it meant facing the unknown horrors of the moon.

The launch was seamless. As the Soyuz rocket pierced the atmosphere, Natalia looked out at the receding Earth, a pale blue marble against the inky blackness of space. She felt a mix of excitement and dread. She was heading into the unknown, into a place where the laws of physics seemed to bend and where the whispers of the moon could drive a person mad.

The Lunar Power Station loomed large as they approached, a cluster of metallic structures clinging to the desolate lunar landscape. As they entered the station, Natalia felt a chill run down her spine, a sense of unease that settled deep within her bones.

The first few days were uneventful. Routine maintenance checks, equipment repairs, radiation monitoring. But Natalia couldn't shake the feeling that they were being watched, that something was lurking just beyond the periphery of their vision.

She began to discreetly investigate the station, searching for the hidden chamber that Dr. Wu Shin had mentioned. She reviewed the schematics, questioned the technicians, and explored every nook and cranny of the complex.
On the fifth day, she found it. Hidden behind a false wall in a rarely used section of the station, she discovered a heavily fortified door, its surface smooth and unmarked. There was no visible lock, no keypad, no indication of how to open it.

Driven by an insatiable curiosity, Natalia spent the next few hours trying to unlock the door. She scanned it with her instruments, analyzed its composition, searched for hidden mechanisms. Finally, she discovered a series of faint symbols etched into the door's surface, symbols that matched the ones Dr. Wu Shin had described.

She carefully transcribed the symbols and fed them into the station's computer. After a tense few minutes, the computer beeped, confirming the sequence. With a low hum, the door slid open, revealing a dark, cavernous chamber.

Natalia hesitated for a moment, her heart pounding in her chest. She didn't know what awaited her inside, but she knew she had to see it. She took a deep breath and stepped into the darkness.

The chamber was vast and silent, illuminated only by a faint, pulsating glow emanating from the center of the room. As Natalia's eyes adjusted, she saw it: a massive crystal, pulsating with an eerie energy, its surface covered in intricate carvings.

She moved closer, drawn to the crystal like a moth to a flame. As she reached out to touch it, a voice echoed in her mind, a clear, resonant voice that seemed to bypass her ears and speak directly to her thoughts.

"Welcome, Natalia Sharma," the voice said. "We have been waiting for you."

Natalia recoiled in shock, her hand hovering just above the crystal. "Who are you? What is this place?"

"We are the keepers of this moon," the voice replied. "This crystal is our heart, our soul. And the Lunar Power Station… it is our tomb."

The crystal pulsed with increased intensity, bathing the chamber in an ethereal light. Natalia felt a rush of images flooding her mind: visions of an ancient civilization, of a world bathed in moonlight, of a terrible war that shattered their society and left them trapped within the moon.

"The uranium is not just fuel," the voice explained. "It is a key. It amplifies our energy, allowing us to communicate, to influence the minds of those who come here."

Natalia finally understood. The memory loss, the hallucinations, the strange behavior… it was all caused by the crystal, by the ancient lunar beings who were desperately trying to escape their prison.

"Why are you telling me this?" she asked.
"Because you are different," the voice said. "You possess a strength of mind, a curiosity, a compassion that the others lacked. We believe you can help us."

Natalia was faced with an impossible choice. She could report her findings, shut down the Lunar Power Station, and condemn the world to an energy crisis. Or she could help the lunar beings escape their prison, potentially unleashing an unknown force upon the Earth.

She looked at the crystal, at the ancient symbols carved into its surface. She felt a surge of empathy for these trapped beings, for their longing for freedom. But she also understood the potential consequences of her actions.

The fate of the Earth, and perhaps the entire solar system, rested on her shoulders. The Lunar Power Station was more than just a power plant; it was a prison, a gateway, and a testament to the enduring mysteries of the universe. And Natalia Sharma, a doctor of Indian descent, was about to decide its fate. This was not just a mystery; it was a cosmic reckoning.

19. THE LUNAR WHISPER – PART TWO

It was Natalia's conviction that the moon held the key to solving Earth's energy crisis. Her research, initially met with skepticism, had demonstrated the viability of harnessing Helium-3, a rare isotope abundant on the lunar surface, to create a clean and virtually limitless source of fusion power. She had been the driving force behind the international coalition that funded the construction of the Lunar Power Station, a massive facility nestled within the Shackleton Crater, perpetually bathed in sunlight.

But now, something was amiss. Whispers of anomalies, of inexplicable energy fluctuations emanating from the station, had reached the ears of those in power. And those whispers had led to a clandestine meeting in Beijing.

Dr. Wu Shin, a man with eyes as sharp and cold as polished jade, rose from his leather chair, his voice a low murmur that barely reached General Zhang's ears.

"The plan, General, is progressing as anticipated. Dr. Sharma has been… misled. The illusion is holding."

General Zhang, a man whose face betrayed nothing, simply nodded. "The Americans and the Europeans are already wavering. Their reports mirror Sharma's observations. They are losing faith in the station."

"Indeed," Dr. Wu Shin agreed. "The crystal pulsed with increased intensity, bathing the chamber in an ethereal light, just as we designed. It's a masterful illusion, carefully calibrated to influence her perceptions. She will, in turn, persuade the others to abandon the main power station, leaving the field clear for us."

The "us," of course, referred to China. They had secretly constructed a standby nuclear power station, a hidden behemoth burrowed deep beneath the lunar surface. It was their contingency plan, their ace in the hole. If the international effort failed, they would seize the opportunity to dominate the lunar resources.

Back on the moon, the Luna-7 crew was settling into their routine. Dimitri oversaw the station maintenance, Anya monitored the life support systems, Boris explored the surrounding crater, and Sergei ensured constant communication with mission control. Natalia, however, was preoccupied. The anomalies she had detected were more pronounced here, inside the power station itself. She felt it in the vibrations under her feet, saw it in the flickering lights, a subtle dissonance that resonated deep within her.

One day, during a routine inspection of the main reactor core, Natalia stopped dead in her tracks. The chamber was bathed in an unnatural, iridescent light. The air shimmered, and the readings on her instruments spiked erratically. This was not the steady hum of a fusion reactor. This was something else entirely, something… artificial.

She approached cautiously, her hand hovering over the emergency release switch on her suit. The light pulsed rhythmically, casting long, distorted shadows across the chamber. It felt almost hypnotic, drawing her in, whispering promises of limitless energy.

Natalia knew, with chilling certainty, that what she was seeing was not real. It was an illusion, a carefully crafted deception designed to mask something far more sinister.

Feigning ignorance, she diligently recorded her observations, noting the intensity, frequency, and spectral analysis of the light. She relayed her findings to Earth, carefully modulating her voice to sound as if she believed everything she was seeing. She knew that somewhere, someone was listening, someone who wanted her to believe the lie.

But Natalia had a plan of her own. Using a highly sensitive gravimetric pulse detector, an instrument designed to map the lunar subsurface, she began scanning for unusual energy signatures beyond the immediate vicinity of the power station. She focused on the far side of the moon, a region largely unexplored, shrouded in perpetual darkness.

Days turned into weeks, and the tension within Luna-7 grew palpable. The other crew members, sensing Natalia's unease, began to question her judgment. Dimitri, ever the pragmatist, urged her to focus on the mission parameters. Anya, the engineer, pointed out the inconsistencies in her data. Even Boris, the jovial geologist, expressed his concerns.

But Natalia remained steadfast. She had a hunch, a gut feeling that something was terribly wrong. And then, she got it. A faint but unmistakable signal, emanating from deep beneath the lunar surface, on the far side of the moon. A heat signature, powerful and concentrated, like nothing she had ever seen.

It was another power station much larger than the original one..

The realization hit her like a physical blow. China. It had to be China. They had built a secret facility, a hidden arsenal of nuclear power, waiting to usurp the international effort.
That night, under the pretense of conducting maintenance on the external sensors, Natalia

slipped away from the habitat. She left a brief message for her crewmates, explaining her suspicions and urging them to trust her. Then, armed with her gravimetric pulse detector and a specialized heat-insulating suit, she set off across the desolate lunar landscape, towards the dark side of the moon.

The journey was arduous, a grueling test of her physical and mental endurance. She navigated treacherous craters, scaled towering mountains, and crossed vast plains of lunar dust. The silence was absolute, broken only by the rhythmic hiss of her oxygen tank and the pounding of her heart.

Finally, she reached her destination. A nondescript plateau, devoid of any distinguishing features. But Natalia knew that beneath the surface, a secret lay hidden.

She activated her gravimetric pulse detector and began scanning the area. The signal grew stronger, leading her towards a barely perceptible crack in the lunar crust. It was a hidden entrance, camouflaged with masterful precision.

As she approached the fissure, she was met by a contingent of robotic security drones. They emerged from the shadows, their metallic bodies gleaming in the faint starlight. They were armed with energy weapons, programmed to defend the facility at all costs.

Natalia knew she couldn't fight them head-on. She activated her heat-insulating suit, creating a localized thermal distortion field that rendered her invisible to the robots' heat sensors. She moved stealthily, weaving through the robotic sentinels, her heart pounding in her chest.

She reached the entrance and slipped inside. The fissure opened into a vast, underground complex, a labyrinth of tunnels and chambers. And at its heart, she found it.

The Chinese nuclear power station. It was even larger and more sophisticated than she had imagined. Reactors hummed with barely contained energy, generators whirred, and technicians, clad in identical Mao suits, scurried about, oblivious to her presence.

Natalia knew she had to act quickly. She contacted her crewmates, relaying her findings and requesting immediate assistance. Dimitri, Anya, Boris, and Sergei, initially shocked and skeptical, quickly rallied to her cause. They understood the gravity of the situation and pledged their unwavering support.

Under Natalia's guidance, the Luna-7 crew launched a daring plan to sabotage the Chinese power station. They planted fusion bombs in strategic locations throughout the facility, targeting the reactors, generators, and control systems. They also created a series of illusioned videos, using advanced holographic technology, depicting the power station as being safe and secure. These videos were designed to mislead the Chinese, buying them time to escape.

As the fusion bombs armed, Natalia and her crew gathered in the main control room. They prepared to initiate the countdown, knowing that the explosion would trigger a chain reaction that would destroy the facility.

But there was one more task to complete. In a hidden chamber, they discovered the remains of previous lunar missions, astronauts who had disappeared without a trace, their bodies preserved in cryogenic stasis. Natalia and her crew recovered the remains, vowing to return them to Earth and give them a proper burial.

With the fusion bombs armed, the illusioned videos activated, and the remains of the fallen astronauts secured, Natalia initiated the countdown. The station began to shake violently as the reactors reached critical mass.

The Luna-7 crew raced back to their lunar lander, launching just as the Chinese power station erupted in a blinding inferno. The explosion reverberated across the lunar surface, a testament to the audacity and sacrifice of a small group of individuals who dared to challenge a global superpower.

As they soared back towards Earth, Natalia looked back at the moon, a single tear tracing a path down her cheek. They had exposed the truth, averted a potential global crisis, and honored the memory of those who had come before them. They had saved the moon, and perhaps, in doing so, they had saved humanity as well. The mystery of the moon's secret power station was solved, but the implications of their discovery would resonate for generations to come.

20. JP SIR – RISE AND FALL

My story begins not in Kerala, the land of my ancestors, but on the shimmering shores of the Andaman Islands. I am Sree Kala, the only daughter, a distinction that came with equal parts love and sorrow. My brothers, strong and agile, could climb coconut trees and chase after crabs with boundless energy. But I, hampered by a leg that refused to cooperate, found my world a little smaller. Yet, within that contained space, my father made sure I felt boundless love. He read me stories of faraway lands, his voice a soothing balm against the sting of exclusion. He saw not my limitations, but the spirit that burned bright within me, a spirit nurtured by the island's turquoise waters and the scent of frangipani that filled the air. I loved the islands with a fierce passion, a love that surpassed any ancestral pull towards Kerala.

Then came Jayaprakash.

I remembered him from my childhood, a playful companion, a familiar face in the small island community. But he was just Jayaprakash, the boy who could run faster, climb higher, and swim deeper than anyone else. Romance was a foreign concept, a seed that hadn't yet sprouted in my young heart. He was studying to be a physical education teacher, a profession that seemed perfectly suited to his imposing physique. He was everything I wasn't: tall, athletic, and radiating a vibrant energy.

When the proposal came, arranged in the traditional way, I was bewildered. Jayaprakash? Why me? He was the catch, the one every girl dreamt of. I was… well, I was just Sree Kala.
But he saw something in me, something that even I hadn't recognized. Perhaps it was the quiet strength I had cultivated, the unwavering spirit that refused to be extinguished by circumstance. Perhaps it was simply kindness. Whatever it was, he wanted me.

Our marriage was a quiet affair, witnessed by the swaying palms and the watchful eyes of the Andaman Sea. I was a short, stout bride, a stark contrast to the magnificent figure of my husband. Yet, as he slipped the thaali around my neck, I felt a sense of peace settle within me, a sense of belonging I hadn't anticipated.

And then, the miracle happened. He loved me. With a depth and intensity that surprised even himself. He treated me with a tenderness that bordered on reverence, his strong hands gentle as he helped me navigate the uneven terrain of the islands. He made me feel beautiful, desirable, worthy. More than my parents, he cherished me.

Lord Murugan blessed us with two daughters, Achu and Nidhi, born two years apart. Our family became the center of my universe. Jayaprakash, the physical education teacher, the man with the commanding presence, was also the father who braided his daughters' hair with clumsy but loving hands, who told them bedtime stories in a booming voice that always ended in giggles, who held them close when they were scared.

His job took us to different islands within the archipelago. Each transfer meant uprooting our lives, but I embraced the change. I was a B.Ed graduate, and finding a teaching position was never a problem. We built a life of simple joys, surrounded by the beauty of the islands and the boundless love within our family.

Jayaprakash was a man who commanded respect. His upright posture, his broad shoulders, his confident stride – he was often mistaken for a police officer, especially in crowded places like airports. He reveled in the attention, a quiet pride swelling in his chest.

I even felt flicker of jealousy watching the Bengali women during Holi. They would purposefully come to our home, their faces flushed with laughter, and smear colour on his cheeks, lingering a little too long, their eyes sparkling with admiration. He was oblivious, of course, his attention solely on me and our daughters. And yet, the seed of insecurity would sprout momentarily, only to be quickly smothered by the overwhelming love and security I felt within our marriage.

Life was good. Almost too good.

Then the storm clouds gathered, slowly at first, almost imperceptibly.

It started with Achu. One day, she fainted on her way home from school. The initial tests revealed nothing alarming, but a persistent doctor ordered a more thorough blood analysis. The diagnosis came as a thunderclap: leukemia.
Our world shattered. The vibrant colours of the islands seemed to fade, replaced by a somber gray. Jayaprakash, my strong, unwavering husband, began to crumble. He started drinking heavily, the golden liquid offering a temporary escape from the unbearable pain. His earnings, once carefully budgeted for our future, were now poured into Achu's treatment in Kerala. We made countless trips to the mainland, our hope dwindling with each passing visit.

While we were stationed in Rangat, fate dealt another cruel blow. A phone call, terse and cold, informed me that Jayaprakash had been in an accident. A fractured hip.

The next six months were a blur of hospital visits and agonizing worry. He recovered, but the man who emerged from the ordeal was a shadow of his former self. The fracture had healed poorly, leaving him with a permanent limp. His posture, once so erect and proud, was now stooped and hesitant. His savings vanished, swallowed by medical bills and his relentless drinking. The man I knew was fading. He was still kind, still loving, but the light within him had dimmed.

We were transferred to Port Blair, closer to the mainland, making it easier for Achu to receive treatment. But the universe seemed determined to test the limits of our endurance.

One day, Nidhi complained of pain in her leg. The diagnosis was swift and brutal: bone cancer, another form of leukemia, attacking the bone above her ankle. She underwent surgery to remove a portion of the affected bone, replaced with a steel plate. Our hearts, already bruised and battered, threatened to break completely.

Months passed, filled with the constant worry that I couldn't give enough time and support to both children equally, as well as my husband. Then, Jayaprakash started experiencing abdominal swelling, a sign of something ominous brewing within him. We rushed him to G.B. Pant Hospital. They drained liters of ascitic fluid from his abdomen, liquid proof of the damage his years of heavy drinking had inflicted. His legs were swollen, his skin stretched taut. Diabetes and kidney failure were rapidly claiming his life.

That night, I stayed with Nidhi at the hospital. I needed to go home, just for a few hours, to freshen up and bring her clean clothes. I left him in Nidhi's care.

That was the end of my happiness.

A phone call shattered the quiet of our home. Nidhi's voice, raw with grief, pierced my heart. "Amma," she sobbed, "Appa is gone."

Jayaprakash was gone. Just like that. His life force, once so vibrant, extinguished by disease and despair.

I rushed back to the hospital, my legs moving on autopilot. I saw his lifeless body, his face gaunt and pale, the proud chest now still. It was over. Everything was over.

His brothers arrived from Kerala to oversee the funeral. They were kind and supportive, but their presence only amplified the gaping hole Jayaprakash had left in our lives.

A year has passed. I still live in Port Blair, surrounded by the familiar beauty of the islands. I live with his memories, clinging to them like precious jewels in a vast ocean of sorrow. I am blessed with my two daughters, my two gems, Achu and Nidhi. Their smiles are my solace, their strength my inspiration. My aged father, a silent pillar of support, reminds me of the enduring power of family.

Life goes on, as it always does. For some, it's filled with vibrant colours and boundless joy. For others, like me, it's a tapestry woven with threads of memory, a bittersweet blend of happiness and profound loss. I will always be grateful for the years I had with Jayaprakash, a man who flourished once, a man who loved me with his whole being, a man whose life, though tragically cut short, left an indelible mark on my heart. His decline was a slow, agonizing process, but his love remains, an eternal flame that guides me through the darkness.

cut short, left an indelible mark on my heart. His decline was a slow, agonizing process,

21. ZUBAIDHA: AN ANDAMAN ELEGY

The wind in this island village, perpetually moist and laden with the scent of salt and blooming mangroves, whispered secrets through the paddy fields of Namunaghar. These fields, a vibrant green carpet under the unforgiving Andaman sun, were the lifeblood of Akram Khan's family, and the defining landscape of Zubaidha's existence. Born the sixth of ten siblings – five brothers and five sisters – Zubaidha was, in many ways, an anomaly. While her siblings sought respite from the sun, dreaming of easier lives away from the mud and toil, Zubaidha found solace and purpose working alongside her father.

Akram Khan was a man of the earth, his hands gnarled and strong, his face etched with the wisdom of seasons past. He saw in Zubaidha a kindred spirit, a daughter who understood the rhythm of the land, the silent language of rice stalks swaying in the breeze. He taught her the art of planting, the patience of weeding, the joy of harvest. The sun painted her skin a rich, dark hue, a badge of honor she wore proudly, a stark contrast to the fairer complexions coveted by her sisters.

Her childhood was a tapestry woven with the earthy scent of paddy, the rhythmic splash of water buffaloes, and the comforting presence of her father. It was during this time, at the tender age of twelve, that Abdul Karim entered her life. He was a vision of youthful charm, fair-skinned and handsome, seeking the hand of Zubaidha's elder sister. But the elder sister, with aspirations beyond the fields of Namunaghar, rejected his proposal. Akram Khan, a man of his word, noticing Zubaidha's innocent admiration for the young man, promised Abdul her hand when she came of age.

From that day forward, Abdul Karim occupied a special place in Zubaidha's young heart. He became the sun around which her world revolved. He was a promise, a hope, a whispered secret she guarded fiercely. Proposals came and went, suitors drawn by the promise of a hardworking bride and a share in Akram Khan's land. But Zubaidha refused them all, her heart already pledged to the absent Abdul, a silent sentinel guarding the flame of first love.

Years passed. Zubaidha blossomed from a girl into a woman, her dark eyes reflecting the unwavering devotion that burned within. When she was fourteen, Abdul Karim returned. The marriage was a simple affair, a joyous celebration held under the watchful gaze of the Andaman stars. Zubaidha felt complete, finally united with the man she had dreamt of for so long.

Their first child, a daughter named Rehana, arrived the following year. Abdul was besotted, Rehana became the center of his universe. He would return from his fishing trips, his hands rough and calloused, and insist on frying the fish himself, feeding Rehana with tender devotion. A second daughter, Rukshana, followed two years later. While the love for Rehana remained undiminished, a subtle shift began to occur in Abdul.

As Zubaidha carried their third child, a storm began brewing in their small household. Abdul started drinking heavily, often disappearing for days, leaving Zubaidha to worry and fend for her growing family. Akram Khan, upon discovering Abdul with another woman at a local liquor shop, was deeply troubled. He was a simple farmer, not equipped to confront his son-in-law's failings. He chose silence, a silence born of helplessness and a desperate prayer that Allah would guide Abdul back to the right path.

Sometimes, Abdul would vanish for months, leaving Zubaidha to shoulder the entire burden of survival. She turned to her father's fields, finding strength in the familiar toil, the rhythmic cycle of planting and harvesting providing a solace amidst the rising tide of despair. She worked tirelessly, her hands becoming rougher, her back aching, her womb swelling with another child. She was perpetually pregnant, a silent testament to the fleeting moments of connection with a man who was increasingly becoming a stranger. Now pregnant with her sixth child, Abdul never returned. She was going to have a child without a husband by her side.

The news, when it finally arrived, shattered the fragile hope she had been clinging to. Abdul, she learned, was planning to marry another woman. The pain was a physical blow, a crushing weight that threatened to suffocate her. But even in the face of such betrayal, the embers of her childhood love for him flickered. She remembered the handsome young man who had knelt before her father, the promise in his eyes, the hope he had ignited in her young heart.

Abandoned and heartbroken, Zubaidha retreated to a small hut at the edge of the paddy fields. Alone, she faced the relentless monsoons of the Andaman Islands, the howling winds mirroring the turmoil within. Her only companions were her six children and a battery-operated radio, from which she listened to old melancholic songs, each melody a painful reminder of what she had lost.

She toiled relentlessly, the paddy fields her only source of sustenance. She taught her children to work the land, instilling in them the same love and respect for the earth that her father had instilled in her. Poverty was a constant companion, but she refused to seek help from her siblings, preferring to maintain her dignity, even in the face of abject hardship. Instead, she shared her meager harvest with them, her generosity a testament to her unwavering spirit.

Years of hard labor, coupled with the emotional strain, took their toll. Zubaidha was diagnosed with high blood sugar, which soon led to kidney failure. Her children, now grown, took turns caring for her, ferrying her to and from the hospital, their faces etched with worry. Though still relatively young, life had aged her prematurely, etching deep lines on her face and stealing the light from her eyes.

Yet, even as her body weakened, her spirit remained unbroken, fueled by the lingering embers of her first love. She waited, with a quiet desperation that only those who have loved and lost can understand, for Abdul to return. She yearned for a glimpse of his face, a word of forgiveness, any sign that he remembered the young girl who had given him her heart so freely.

One stormy night, as the wind howled and the rain lashed against the windows of her small hut, Zubaidha began to struggle for breath. Her children rushed her towards the hospital, their faces illuminated by the flickering light of the kerosene lamp. But it was too late. On the way, cradled in her third daughter's arms, Zubaidha breathed her last.

News of her death spread quickly through Namunaghar and beyond. Relatives and friends from across the Andaman Islands came to pay their last respects, their faces etched with sorrow and regret. But amid the weeping and mourning, one person was conspicuously absent: Abdul Karim.

Zubaidha was laid to rest in the Noor Masjid burial ground in Namunaghar, the earth damp from the relentless rain. As the mourners dispersed, and the wind continued its mournful song, one could almost feel her spirit hovering over the grave, a silent question hanging in the air. What had she done wrong? Why hadn't he come, even to see her lifeless body one last time?

And so, Zubaidha, the peasant girl of Namunaghar, rests in her grave, forever awaiting the return of her beloved Abdul, her soul forever bound to the land she loved and the man who broke her heart. The paddy fields of Namunaghar, once vibrant with the promise of life, now stand as a silent testament to a love betrayed, a life of hardship, and a spirit that, even in death, continues to yearn for what might have been. The wind whispers her name through the swaying rice stalks, a mournful elegy for a life lived and a love lost, forever etched in the heart of the Andaman Islands.

22. THASOS – BLOOD AND STONE

From the ashes of a fallen age, where gods still whispered in the rustling olive groves and the clang of bronze echoed through sun-drenched lands, comes the tale of Baricos of Thasos, a man forged in the crucible of love and loss, a legend etched in blood.

Baricos, they called him the Bear of Kastro. A man sculpted from the very mountains of Thasos, his muscles rippled with the strength of a demigod, his eyes held the clear, fierce light of the Aegean sun. Amongst the men of Kastro, he stood tall, a champion undefeated in the games, a protector against the petty squabbles that plagued the fractured Greek kingdoms. He was a man content, until the day his gaze fell upon Tiara of Theologos.

The monthly market, a bustling tapestry of sights and smells, was a lifeline for the islanders. It was there, amidst the haggling merchants and the bleating sheep, that Baricos saw her. Tiara. Her beauty was a radiant bloom in the dusty square, her dark hair cascading like a silken waterfall, her eyes, pools of liquid amber, held a spark that could ignite a thousand sunsets. Some whispered she was touched by Aphrodite herself, too glorious for mortal hands. Indeed she carried herself with such grace that the village folk said only Staphylus, the young God of Wine, was worthy of her beauty.

Baricos, normally unmoved by such ethereal notions, was struck dumb. His heart, a sturdy fortress, crumbled before her smile. He was a warrior, a protector, but in that moment, he was simply a man, captivated by a woman.

But Thasos, though Greek in spirit, was a pawn in the game of empires. The Romans, with their insatiable hunger for conquest and their thirst for spectacle, arrived yearly, their ships heavy with shackles and their pockets lined with silver, buying and selling lives like mere commodities. Men for the brutal arena, women for their twisted pleasures. While overt plunder was kept at bay through trade agreements with the Greek king, the air crackled with unspoken tension.

One fateful market day, that tension snapped. A slave woman, desperate and driven by the primal instinct for freedom, burst from the hold of a Roman ship, her screams piercing the vibrant air. Philipos, a Roman commander with a face as hard as granite and eyes as cold as a winter sea, and his men gave chase, swords glinting menacingly.

The woman, in her blind flight, stumbled before Baricos. The crowd recoiled, fear etching lines on their faces. No one dared defy Rome. But Baricos, his heart ignited by the injustice and the terror in the woman's eyes, stepped forward.

"Let her go," he commanded, his voice a low rumble that silenced the market.

The Roman soldiers, contemptuous of the islanders, sneered. Their reply was the clang of steel as they dragged the woman towards the ship. Baricos, his patience exhausted, unleashed the fury within. He moved with the speed and power of a storm, a whirlwind of fists and fury. Six Roman soldiers fell before him, bruised and battered, their pride shattered. The slave woman, trembling and bewildered, was freed.

Philipos, enraged by this defiance, confronted Baricos, his voice dripping with venom. "You dare interfere with Roman law? You will pay for this insolence!"

Baricos, his eyes blazing, roared back, "This is not Rome! This is Thasos! Take your chains and your cruelty elsewhere!"

Philipos, momentarily stunned by the raw power emanating from the islander, retreated to his ship, but not without a chilling promise of retribution.

It was in the aftermath of this defiance, this raw display of courage, that Tiara saw Baricos for who he truly was. Not just a strong man, but a righteous one. And Baricos, emboldened by her admiration, saw in her eyes a love that mirrored his own.

The courtship was swift and ardent. Baricos, with the blessings of his village, arrived at Theologos, his presence a promise of protection and devotion. The villagers welcomed him with open arms, and plans for a wedding were set.

The week that followed was a whirlwind of joyous preparations. The air thrummed with the scent of roasting lamb and the lilting melodies of traditional songs. As the wedding day dawned, the villages of Kastro and Theologos were united in celebration. But far away, in the heart of Rome, Philipos was plotting his vengeance. Exploiting the internal strife plaguing the Greek kingdoms, he secured permission from Caesar to unleash a brutal attack on Thasos.

As the sun dipped below the horizon, casting long shadows across the festive scene, the first Roman ships appeared on the horizon, their silhouettes dark and ominous against the fiery sky. Panic erupted as the ships began to bombard the port, catapulting flaming projectiles that ignited the merchant vessels, turning the harbor into a raging inferno.

The Roman legions swarmed ashore, a tide of steel and savagery. They cut down anyone who resisted, their swords dripping with the blood of innocent men, women, and children. The whispers of laughter were replaced by screams of terror, the scent of celebration drowned in the stench of burning flesh. Thasos, once a haven of peace, was plunged into a night of unspeakable horror.

Baricos, hearing the chaos, raced through the burning streets of Kastro, his heart pounding with dread. He found Tiara, huddled and terrified, and entrusted her to the protection of his loyal friend, Simpos. Then, with a roar of primal rage, he plunged into the fray, a one-man army against the Roman onslaught. He was a force of nature, a whirlwind of death, cutting down Roman soldiers with each swing of his heavy axe.

But Philipos, driven by his desire for revenge and his lust for Tiara, was relentless. He learned of Tiara's whereabouts and descended upon Simpos's home with his soldiers. Simpos, along with his family, was butchered, and Tiara was dragged away, her screams echoing in the night.

News of Tiara's abduction reached Baricos, fueling his already unimaginable rage. He fought his way to the port, unaware that Tiara was being used as a bait to trap him. As he reached the docks, he was surrounded by hundreds of Roman soldiers. A net, weighted with stones, was cast upon him, ensnaring him in its suffocating embrace. He was beaten mercilessly, the Roman soldiers reveling in the humiliation of the man who had dared to defy them.

Bound and battered, he was dragged before Philipos, where he saw Tiara chained to a mast, her eyes filled with terror and despair. "Spare her! Take my life instead!" he begged, his voice raw with anguish. But Philipos only laughed, his eyes gleaming with cruel satisfaction.

Baricos blacked out, the last sound he heard being Tiara's desperate screams.

He awoke to a scene of unimaginable desolation. The port was a graveyard, littered with corpses and smoldering wreckage. The air hung thick with the stench of death. As his eyes focused, he saw a crow perched upon a figure slumped against the mast. It was Tiara. Lifeless. Her once vibrant eyes were now vacant, her beautiful face contorted in silent horror.

A primal scream tore from Baricos's throat, a sound that echoed across the ravaged island, a sound that carried on the wind like a curse. He cursed Philipos, he cursed Rome, he cursed the gods themselves for their indifference.

"Philipos!" he roared, his voice filled with a grief that could shatter mountains. "Your fate... is now sealed by Baricos of Thasos!"

His legend was not over. It was just beginning. This wasn't a battlefield he was in but a colosseum now. He was captured and taken on the roman ship for a show, a gladiator. The games were a show of force and entertainment in Rome. The champion of Thasos was now chained, but the spark of vengeance still burned bright in his eyes, a promise of inevitable retribution, a legend ready to be reborn in the blood-soaked sands of the arena. His fate would be decided by his own hands, not by the whims of gods or the cruelty of men. The Bear of Thasos would have his day.

23. LIFE – A GIFT TO BE LIVED

The flickering gas lamp cast long, distorted shadows across the cluttered room, painting a grim tableau of Inder's despair. He lay sprawled on the worn rug, the crimson stain blooming across the threadbare fibers like a malevolent flower. The air hung thick with the metallic tang of blood and the cloying sweetness of cheap liquor.

Inder was a man adrift, a solitary vessel tossed about on a turbulent sea of loss. At 45, his hair was already streaked with silver, reflecting the grey landscape of his soul. He was a shadow of the vibrant man he once was, a man full of laughter and dreams, a man who had believed in the promise of life.

The observer saw this scene unfolding, a silent witness to Inder's agony. He saw the tremor in Inder's hand as he'd gripped the razor, the grimset line of his mouth, the haunted look in his eyes. He saw the brief flicker of hesitation before the blade sliced into his wrist, the almost immediate regret that followed.

Why had Inder arrived at this desolate crossroads? The story of his unraveling was etched into the very lines on his face, a narrative of love lost, dreams shattered, and a soul slowly eroded by grief.

Ten years ago, Inder had been a different man. He was a successful architect, his designs gracing the city skyline. He had a loving wife, Priya, whose laughter was the soundtrack to his life, and a bright, inquisitive daughter, Anya, who was the center of his universe. He had it all, or so it seemed.

Then, tragedy struck with the force of a rogue wave. A drunk driver, speeding through a red light, stole Priya and Anya from him in an instant. The vibrant colors of Inder's world faded to monochrome. The laughter was replaced by an echoing silence that haunted his waking hours and invaded his dreams.

He tried to cope. He threw himself into his work, burying his grief beneath blueprints and concrete. But the buildings he designed felt hollow, devoid of the life and joy they were meant to house. Every curve, every line, reminded him of the curves of Priya's smile, the lines of Anya's delicate features.

He started drinking, a slow slide into oblivion fueled by self-pity and a desperate need to numb the pain. He lost clients, lost his reputation, lost his will to live. His once-meticulously ordered apartment became a reflection of his inner chaos, a repository of empty bottles and forgotten memories.

His friends tried to reach out, offering condolences and support, but Inder pushed them away. He couldn't bear to see their pity, couldn't bear to talk about the void that had consumed him. He felt like a leper, contagious with his grief, and he didn't want to infect anyone else.

He became a recluse, a ghost in his own life. He spent his days wandering the streets, a silent observer of the world he no longer felt a part of. He'd sit for hours in the park where he used to take Anya, watching other fathers play with their children, a sharp pang of longing twisting in his gut.

The anniversary of Priya and Anya's death was always the hardest. He would lock himself in his apartment, surrounded by their photographs, and drink until he passed out. This year, however, was different. This year, the grief felt unbearable, a crushing weight that threatened to suffocate him.

He had spent days in a stupor, barely eating, barely sleeping, haunted by vivid memories of happier times. He replayed their last day together in his mind, trying to find some sign, some warning, some way he could have prevented the tragedy. He found none.

And so, he had decided to end it. To join Priya and Anya in whatever afterlife awaited them. He imagined them waiting for him, their faces wreathed in smiles, their arms outstretched in welcome. It was the only solace he could find.
But fate, it seemed, had other plans. The observer watched as Inder lay bleeding, his breathing shallow and erratic. He saw the first signs of hypothermia setting in, the telltale shivering despite the warm blood

seeping into the rug. He saw the life slowly ebbing away.

Then, a sound. A faint, persistent knocking at the door.

Inder, unconscious, didn't hear it. The observer, a mere witness, could do nothing to alert him. The knocking continued, growing more insistent. Finally, the door rattled, then creaked open.

A young woman stood in the doorway, her face etched with concern. Her name was Maya, and she lived in the apartment below Inder's. She had noticed the increasingly pungent smell emanating from his place and hadn't seen him in days. Driven by a growing sense of unease, she had finally decided to investigate.

She stepped into the apartment, her eyes widening in horror at the scene before her. She rushed to Inder's side, her hands trembling as she checked for a pulse. Faint, but present.

Without hesitation, she grabbed her phone and called for help. She applied pressure to the wounds on his wrists, desperately trying to stem the flow of blood. She spoke to him in soothing tones, even though he couldn't hear her, telling him to hold on, that help was on the way.

The ambulance arrived with sirens wailing, shattering the silence of the night. Paramedics rushed into the apartment, their movements swift and efficient. They stabilized Inder and whisked him away to the hospital, leaving Maya standing alone in the blood-soaked apartment, shaking with adrenaline.

Inder spent the next few days in intensive care, hovering between life and death. He survived, but the experience left him shaken and vulnerable. He woke up feeling not relief, but a deep sense of shame and regret.

Maya visited him in the hospital, her presence a silent testament to the kindness of strangers. She didn't judge him, didn't preach to him, didn't offer platitudes about moving on. She simply sat with him, her quiet empathy a balm to his wounded soul.

As Inder recovered, he began to see the world with new eyes. He realized that he had been so consumed by his grief that he had become blind to the beauty and goodness that still existed in the world. He saw Maya's compassion, the dedication of the nurses, the unwavering support of his few remaining friends.

He started therapy, slowly peeling back the layers of pain and trauma that had suffocated him for so long. He began to reconnect with his old passions, sketching designs again, finding solace in the creative process. He even started volunteering at a local animal shelter, finding comfort in the unconditional love of the rescued animals.

The scars on his wrists remained, a constant reminder of his darkest hour, but they also served as a symbol of his resilience, his ability to survive even the deepest despair. He would never forget Priya and Anya, but he learned to live with their absence, to honor their memory by living a life filled with purpose and meaning.

The observer watched Inder's transformation with a sense of cautious hope.

He saw the flicker of life returning to his eyes, the faint smile that occasionally graced his lips. He saw a man who had once been lost in the darkness slowly finding his way back to the light.

Inder's story was a testament to the human capacity for both despair and redemption. It was a reminder that even in the face of unimaginable loss, hope can still bloom, that even in the darkest of nights, a single act of kindness can illuminate the path to a new dawn. And finally, sometimes, a little intervention is all that is needed to turn someone away from the abyss.

24. SHADOWS OF LONG ISLAND

The sun dipped low over Long Island, casting golden rays over the serene waters that kissed the shores of Lalaji Bay. This was a sanctuary for Bala, an engineer turned recluse, who had chosen to escape the relentless clutches of his past. With the gentle whisper of the sea breeze, he sat on the sandy beach, his daughter Roja beside him, playing with a small shell she had found. The idyllic setting filled his heart with warmth, yet shadows lingered in his mind.

Bala had lived in this coconut-scented paradise for three years now, but he always felt the weight of his memories pressing against his chest. His tears, he often told Roja, were born from an overwhelming happiness that surged within whenever he saw her laugh. She took his word for it—innocent and trusting. What could she possibly know about the darkness he had left behind?

His life in New Delhi had been a tapestry of brilliance unraveling into chaos. Just before the sudden loss of his wife, he had published a theoretical paper on compact nuclear power that had sparked the interest of many. It was a work that could shine a brilliant light or cast a devastating shadow—his creation had the potential to either illuminate the world with new energy or annihilate it in destruction. To him, parting with it had been the only way to protect Roja. He had destroyed the working model just days before the tragic event, and with it, a part of himself. Now, with her mischief lighting up his world, he had hoped to cultivate a simple life away from the treachery borne of power.

But peace was a fragile thing, and in a world teetering on the edge of conflict, it seldom lasted long.

One evening, as they sat around their makeshift campfire, lighting up the darkness, Roja looked up at him, her eyes twinkling like stars. "Papa, why do sometimes tears fall when you smile?"

He chuckled, his heart heavy yet full. "It's a trick of the heart, Roja. Sometimes we feel everything all at once—happiness, sadness, and love. It all mingles together."

But deep inside, a storm was brewing. Bala's insecurities jumped at the thought of exposing his secret life. His decision to disconnect from the world was predicated on a deep-seated urge for self-preservation and protection for his daughter. Cutting ties with humanity seemed the only escape from the complexities of his past.

In New Delhi, Bala's footsteps had not gone unnoticed. Professor Shailender Sharma, a relentless scholar and a man fascinated by nuclear science, had been tracking him for years. The professor was convinced that Bala still held the key to a groundbreaking innovation that could tilt the balance of power in favor of those who possessed it. That was precisely why he had become a target for many entities, and unbeknownst to Bala, eyeing eyes were lurking in the shadows.

Weeks passed in quietude, but then the storm broke.

The school headmaster in the village made an innocuous error. A mandate required him to upload the admission list for the new term online. And in that instant, Bala's world spiraled once more into chaos. Roja had been accepted into the local school—a cause for celebration, yet instead became their greatest vulnerability.

The ripple effect of this innocuous act alerted authorities in New Delhi. Dr. Wang Shu of the Chinese embassy, always on the lookout for scientific breakthroughs, identified Bala through the admission list as well. News spread through cables and rapid communications, reaching military commanders who felt Bala was a risk they could not afford.

The coast guard received their orders, but Bala was ahead of them. When he discovered his name on that list, a cold sweat dripped down his back. The storm clouds darkened above, and with haste, he made arrangements to leave Long Island. He bought a boat ticket to Rangat Island, planning to fade even further into the depths of the ocean.

But even then, he could feel the long fingers of his past stretching toward him. He had no idea how close those fingers were.

Under the cover of night, with Roja fast asleep in their small, coconut-fringed home, Bala packed their necessities—clothes, food, a small amount of cash, and the only remnant of his wife: a locket containing her picture. He could hear the distant sound of the ocean lapping at the shore, and with it, a sense of urgency enveloped him.

By dawn, he had already set off. But the air buzzed with tension; shadows were moving in the depths of the storm that now brewed across the ocean. Burmese fishermen hired by Dr. Wang had already traced the rumors of his departure and were sent after him.

In Delhi, chaos erupted, with the professor imploring the defense minister to raise the security response on the Andaman Islands. But the minister remained uncompromising, citing the cost of pursuing a single individual. Nonetheless, they raised an alert for the coast guard, warning them of the encroaching darkness being orchestrated by foreign hands.

The fishing boat met with the churning seas as the Chinese Air Force began mobilizing troops from Great Coco Islands. It was an unthinkable confrontation set against the backdrop of a tranquil beach. By the time the coast guard located the fishing boat on the coast of Long Island, it was already too late; the conflict had begun.

As explosions rocked the small island, Bala and Roja sailed westward in the dead of night, unaware of the horror unfolding behind them.

Days turned into weeks, and the clash consumed the north and south islands. The tranquility that had once filled Long Island was replaced with deafening booms and the rumble of distant conflicts. Entire villages were left in ruins as international forces clashed; the conflict overshadowed the truth of what it all began with—an engineer seeking a peaceful life for his child.

But even as the war raged, something powerful had taken root in Bala's heart: an indomitable resolve. With nothing left to lose, he would fight to protect the only family he had left.

Once a recluse, now thrust into a war meant to silence him, he and Roja sailed unnoticed toward Lakshadweep Islands, their new beginning uncertain yet ripe with potential. Breath hitching in his throat, he clung to her hand as she laughed softly in the wind.

"Where are we going, Papa?" she asked, her eyes wide and innocent.

"To a place where the shadows can't find us," he replied, his voice firm yet gentle.

As the sun rose over the horizon, enveloping the ocean in shades of orange and pink, the remnants of their old lives began to fade into the distance. The sea would hide their secrets, and as long as they had each other, they would face whatever storms may come.

In that moment, Bala felt something shift within him. Those tears he once considered burdens were now symbols of both the heartache they left behind and the hope they carried forward, lighting their way into an uncertain future.

THANKING MESSAGE

The last period rests heavy on the page. "Thank you," I wrote, a final, almost perfunctory gesture. And now it's done. The third book, a collection of short stories and some of them are in poetic style, some historical and some biographical but every story is unique in itself.

I glance at the bottom of the last page, where I've left my email and WhatsApp details: balajinadar09@gmail.com and +919791048441. A small, hopeful offering in the form of feed back. I'm not just an author sending a book into the void; I'm reaching out, inviting connection, hoping someone out there will see themselves in these stories as I saw them while writing. It's terrifying and thrilling, this vulnerability. But above all, it's sincere. Thank you, truly, for reading.